Interior
MOTIVES

Interior
MOTIVES

DEADLY DÉCOR MYSTERIES
BOOK 3

Ginny Aiken

Revell
Grand Rapids, Michigan

© 2006 by Ginny Aiken

Published by Fleming H. Revell
a division of Baker Publishing Group
P.O. Box 6287, Grand Rapids, MI 49516-6287
www.revellbooks.com

Printed in the United States of America

Library of Congress Cataloging-in-Publication Data
Aiken, Ginny.
    Interior motives / Ginny Aiken.
        p.   cm. — (Deadly decor mysteries ; bk. 3)
    ISBN 10: 0-8007-3046-1 (pbk.)
    ISBN 978-0-8007-3046-8 (pbk.)
    1. Women interior decorators—Fiction. I. Title.
PS3551.I339I58 2006
813'.54—dc22   2006007967

Published in association with the literary agency of Alive Communications, Inc., 7680 Goddard Street, Suite 200, Colorado Springs, Colorado 80920.

My sheep listen to my voice; I know them, and they follow me.
I give them eternal life, and they shall never perish; no one can
snatch them out of my hand.

John 10:27–28

1

Wilmont, Washington

"Read 'em and weep!"

As if to punctuate the words, documents landed on my kitchen table, just inches away from my innocent nose. I'd been working. My drama-queen neighbor's arrival and declaration put an end to my efforts. She's trouble. Always.

I looked up; I goggled. "Bella?"

"Who'd ya think it was, Haley girl? Marvin the Martian?"

That was a loaded question, even though Marvin didn't come into the mix. I scrambled for an inoffensive answer while I studied her. I could've said Columbo. The Maltese Falcon came to mind too. Even the Pink Panther would've worked. But Bella Cahill? She of the repeated high-speed changes of way crazy hair color and varied hobbies?

Uh-uh.

A fedora rode low over her eyes. Jet black Brillo Pad tufts of hair escaped the hat's confines, a totally weird color

choice for someone who's boasted of Pepto pink and tur-
quoise hair in the last year or so. A tan raincoat hid her
roly-poly bod, her Pillsbury Doughboy curves more dis-
guised by the coat than by the wet suit, martial arts' *gi*, and
spandex bike shorts she's worn in the recent past. Black
sunglasses and brown loafers finished off today's carica-
turelike costume.

"What was I thinking?" I finally offered with a *thwap* to
my forehead. "But I was working, you know."

"You doing design-gig stuff, or are you and the hunky
builder hunting crooks again?"

I stood and did some heavy-duty eye rolling. "Bella, I'm
an interior designer, and you know it. I'm not a detective,
much less a crook hunter, as you put it."

The wacky vision yanked off her glasses to expose a still
beautiful if indignant face. "And what do you call nailing
a couple of killers? Huh?"

I shuddered. "Being at the wrong place at the wrong
time."

"Oh, sure. What shoved you into the scenes of the crimes
was that wrong place wrong time stuff, but cracking two
murder cases doesn't happen just by closing your eyes
and wiggling your nose. You gotta do something to get
somewhere with that kind of slime bucket."

True, but not anything I'd wanted to do in the first
place, and no way do I want to come face-to-face with that
again.

Ever.

Never.

"Enough about me," I said with a wave toward her outfit. "What's that all about?"

She slammed her fists on her abundant hips. "What? You want me to believe you went blind and stupid overnight? You? The chick who figured out whodunit when the cops couldn't? No way, Haley girl. Take a gander at me, and I'm sure you'll get it. If you don't, then just read these."

The documents under her chubby finger looked official, one of them a lot like a license. My gut wriggled with unease. Unease? Scratch unease; ravening fear's more like it around Bella. I picked them up. And groaned.

"What Cracker Jack box did these come from?"

Bella's glare shot off sparks. "I'll have you know I got my training from a real, honest-to-goodness mail-order college. Once I had that, I took a test and got my license."

I gave the documents in my hand a quick scan, stumbled back to my chair, and collapsed. One of my worst nightmares had just come to life. If what I held was as real as Bella said, the state of Washington had licensed her as a PI—private investigator.

Be afraid. Be very afraid.

She scares me, all right. She and her cats.

"Okay," I said. "So what does it mean?"

Bella scoffed and doffed her fedora. "What do you think it means? It means I made my lifelong dream come true. I'm going to follow that dream and use my hidden talents. I'm going to help you bust open cases."

Hidden talents? Help *me* break cases? *Oh boy.*

"Um . . ." What to do? "Ah . . . you might do better if you

. . . ah . . . er . . . oh yeah! Pull an Ace Ventura and become a pet detective. After all, even when you don't do anything, pets flock to you—like your Faux Bali did. You have a knack, a gift. You'll be an overnight success. Trust me."

I said all that with a straight face. A massive feat, since I not only know her cats—the original Bali H'ai and Faux Bali too—but also was present when that second feral feline burst into Bella's life at the most inopportune time—inopportune for me, of course.

Her doubtful look gave me hope—she hadn't rejected my argument outright. So I followed with, "No, really. I think you'll be fabulous. You love critters of all sorts, especially cats, and with your . . . specialized training you can do a whole lot of good. Just imagine how the owners will feel when you return their pets."

And stay out of trouble, while you're at it.

Maybe.

Bella's frown radiated skepticism. "You really think so? That sounds so . . . so unsignifivial."

I blinked. "Insignificant? Trivial?"

"Whatever. You get my drift. That kind of stuff won't make a difference in the greater scheme of things. I want to be"—she drew large, eloquent arm gestures—"relevant."

My golden retriever, Midas, chose that moment to enter the kitchen. I pounced on the opportunity. "How can you call pets trivial? Especially since I know how much you love your two beasts."

Her lips pursed and jutted, her eyes closed, her brain

churned the idea to where I could almost hear the creak of the gears within.

"Well . . . ," she finally said. "Animals are noble creatures. And I do love my Balis—who are *not* beasts, and you know it."

I know no such thing, but she was on a roll, so I let it ride.

"You might be onto something," she conceded. "Maybe I'll go home and pull my ad from the paper. It's only run for three days, and then I can come up with a new one."

She used both thumbs and forefingers to make a frame through which she squinted. "I can just see the sign on my front door. 'Bella Cahill, Pet Detective.' It does kinda have a ring to it."

"Oh! Excuse me," my father said from the doorway.

I looked up, surprised I hadn't heard him arrive. "Hi, Dad. How was your day?"

He dropped a kiss on my mutinous hair. "Typical. But I did finish my sermon for this Sunday."

"Ah," I said. "Productive."

"In that regard." A look swept the counters and the stove. "What's for dinner?"

I winced. "Oops! Sorry. I lost track of time while I worked on the redesign of Tedd Rodriguez's office. Then Bella showed up."

"Bella?" he asked. He gave our guest a closer look. A moment later his eyes widened, and I knew how I must've looked when Washington's newest PI first walked in. "My goodness! It *is* you, isn't it? I wouldn't have known you out on the street."

"Why, thank you, Hale. That's the nicest compliment I've had in ages." She turned to me. "See? I did real well in my disguises class. Even your dad, who's known me for years, didn't recognize me."

Dad frowned. "That's good? I'm afraid I don't understand."

Bella snatched her paperwork from my fingers and gave it to Dad. "Here. This'll tell the story better than I can."

Dad reads fast. "You've become a private investigator? Why?"

"I've had the dream for years," she answered, a blush on her still smooth cheeks. "And since Haley keeps tripping over dead bodies, I figure I have to be ready to help her the next time."

He closed his eyes, and his lips moved in silent communion with the Lord. "I hope and pray there won't be another time. The last two were tough enough."

Dad too was a victim the last time I solved a murder case, and I know how much he'd suffered. His jaw tightened, and sadness etched lines on his forehead.

I blurted, "Would you like to see the drawings for Tedd's office?"

Bella's glare busted me. I didn't get away with my clumsy change of topic unnoticed. "Sure," the new gumshoe said without much enthusiasm.

Dad nodded.

The design for the remodel of my friend's office was

simple, elegant, and flavored with touches of south-of-the-border spice. Hand-tooled leather chairs from Guatemala—which should already have arrived but for some weird shipping reason hadn't yet—would replace the bland beige sofas. Ebonized wood tables, magazines on top, would sit at easy reach for the clients who arrived early for their appointments with the successful psychotherapist. And for that certain zip, Mexican blankets, all in shades of warm brown, terra cotta, taupe, and cream, would cover the pillows I planned to toss here and there.

Bella beamed. "It looks totally rad—that's what kids say, you know."

Dad nodded. "I'm impressed, honey. You do have a gift for this. I'm so thankful you followed through on your schooling."

I rose and gave him a quick hug. "Even when it means dinner's way late?"

"Even then. It's a blessing to see you move ahead with your life."

It was my turn for the rotten memories. A few years ago, I was a victim of violent crime. It took me a long time to crawl out of the pit of despair in the aftermath, but I'm on the upswing now. Dad was there for me, supported me all the way. And Tedd helped lead me back to the Lord I'd blamed.

I shook off the gloom. "Yepper. It is good, Dad. But it won't be very good if we don't eat soon."

Dad looked from me to Bella and back to me. "How about we celebrate Bella's success? Let's go grab something good—Bella's choice."

I scooted behind the euphoric Bella and glared, shook my head, made wild gestures, but my father either didn't understand my pathetic efforts or chose to ignore them—my bet is on the latter. I couldn't believe he was about to encourage the incorrigible septuagenarian in her latest lunacy.

Even though I lost that battle, dinner was great; we had a blast. And I didn't have to deal with Bella's fur wads. Bali and Faux Bali stayed home.

"No, you can't."

I clenched my fists and blew a disobedient curl off my forehead. "Who says?"

All six feet something of Dutch Merrill bristled. "I do. And I'm the contractor."

"So what? I'm the designer. I say the old cookie-cutter, builder's-supply-store doors go, and so they go."

"Listen to me, Farrell. I know you want your funky, antique, hand-carved Mexican doors. And I don't question your design sensibilities. But would you just look at those things for a minute?"

I did. I stared at the gorgeous hundred-plus-year-old mahogany doors with the kind of patina baby-fresh woods envy. "I'm looking, Dutch, and I see the perfect doors for this design—the ones I told you about three weeks ago when they came into the auction house's warehouse. I knew even before that. The minute I opened the email with photos from Ozzie's shopping trip south of the border, I knew they belonged in Tedd's office."

"And I told you back then your assistant might be spinning his wheels, that the doors might not fit the frames. And that's the deal."

"But look at the doors."

"I have. They're to die for. Okay? But I have to live in the present—with these." He pounded the wood trim in the doorway. "Back when those things were carved, no one thought about codes and standards and all those boring things. That doesn't mean I get to ignore them. I have an inspector to face."

"You're the contractor, right? Figure out how to fit them."

"How? You want me to knock the place down, stick the pieces and parts in a time capsule, and zip us back to nineteenth-century Mexico?"

"Hey, if that's what it takes, go for it, Orwell."

I stomped out. All right. I'm not proud of it, but that's just what I did. I stomped like a two-year-old whose mother had whisked her blanky to the wash. But what good is a contractor if he can't do what you need him to do?

True, Dutch works wonders with the budget, comes in on time or earlier, and manages to make ho-hum structures look anything but. Still, I'm the designer, not him.

I want my doors.

Even if they don't fit.

Which is totally unreasonable.

Which is why I had to make a U-turn in the hall of Tedd's office. At one of the doorways in question, I paused.

"Um . . . ah, Dutch?"

"What now?"

Oh boy. That growl didn't bode well for my apology. "I don't blame you for being ticked off at me—"

"Ticked off? Can I trade you in for six normal doors?"

My cheeks turned to the hot side of the color wheel. "I doubt you'll get any takers on that bargain. I know I'd pass."

"Huh?"

I tucked a bunch of wild hair behind my ear, then held out my right hand. "Peace? I know I acted like a brat, and I'm sorry. Please forgive me, and please work with me on the doors."

He stared at my hand as if it were the Trojan horse full of . . . well, stuff as old as the horse for him to stick in the remodel—like the doors. Poor guy.

"Come on, Dutch. I feel really stupid, and we have to work together on this project. Meet me halfway here, will you?"

"Halfway might be too far." He took my hand, yanked me toward him, and added insult to injury by ruffling my already more than ruffled hair. "I can't change code restrictions, and you know it."

I swatted at his hands but landed no swats. He's taller and quicker.

With one hand I shoved my crazy hair out of my eyes, and with the other I smoothed my taupe T-shirt over the waist of my long denim skirt.

"Okay." I could be gracious. "So replacing the doors is out. And halfway—whatever that might mean—is also out. What can we do with the doors? Even you have to admit they're gorgeous."

Dutch stepped toward the troublesome decorative elements, intense concentration on his rugged face. He ran a hand through his dark hair, then pulled out a measuring tape and applied it to one of the doors. He shook his head.

"I can't see how I can use them, Haley."

"There has to be something you can do. They're perfect for the design *and* for Tedd."

"Who's bandying my name?" the gorgeous Latina shrink asked, a half smile on her red-lipsticked mouth. "Are you two at it again?"

"Yes—"

"No—"

She laughed. "I guess there's not much the Merrill and Farrell comedy team can agree on, is there?"

Dutch's eyebrows crashed into his hairline. "Comedy team? I don't think so. It's not so much that we disagree as that Haley hasn't learned that not everything is possible. Sometimes things just don't work. Like here."

I ignored his dumb comment. "So you don't really hate the doors?"

"Weren't you listening? I never said I did."

"You just don't see how to replace the old ones with these."

"Well, these are the old ones, the really old ones, but no. I can't hang these instead of standard doors and stick to code."

The word *hang* caught my attention. Ideas strobed through my head. "What if . . . ? Hey, go with me here, okay? These frames are wider than the doors."

"That's the problem."

Tedd crossed her arms and leaned against the wall, her smile now full-watt bright.

I did some more ignoring, this time of what I suspected Tedd's smile meant, and continued to think out loud. "To stay within code we can't make the doorways narrower."

"Right again—think about Tedd's clients in wheel-chairs."

Another look at the wide hall, which opens to the gener-ous waiting room, and one of the million ideas began to jell. "Of course. But what if . . . ?"

I walked to the waiting room, tapped my lips, and thought some more.

Behind me, Tedd's sharp, high-heeled steps followed Dutch's heavier ones.

"What if . . . ?" Dutch prodded.

My brain buzzed as if on a Starbucks overdose. "I hadn't planned artwork for the hallway, but what if I use the doors as wall art?"

He gave me one of his "Now you've really lost it" looks.

"Now, wait. Hear me out. We all agree the doors are fabulous. And they're historic treasures someone—us—has to save. So if they can't be used in modern construction, why don't we take advantage of their art value? The carv-ing is magnificent."

Tedd headed back to where I'd stacked the doors. She ran a red-tipped finger over the intricate detail, her smile wider by the second.

Dutch joined her.

I followed, certain of my new vision.

Patience is not one of my stronger virtues, and it didn't show any sign of fortification right then. But I bit my tongue and zipped my lip. I waited them out.

When Dutch gave a soft "hmm . . ." I knew I'd won the battle. And, to my credit, I didn't crow.

Instead, I said, "Don't you think small, museumlike halogen spots above each door panel, like the ones I had installed around the perimeter of the waiting room, would make for a dramatic display?"

Dutch began to nod. He whipped out his measuring tape again and nodded some more. "Not only are the doors narrower than the openings, but they're also shorter. That means we should have enough space above them for your spotlights to aim just right. Now, I'll still have to figure out a way to hang them without pulling down the walls—"

"Aw, give me a break, Merrill! I can't believe you're about to throw up another roadblock. That should be a piece of cake for you."

"Yeah, like I can leap tall buildings and stop runaway trains, right?"

I blushed again. "Well, maybe you're not quite Super-man, but you're pretty handy with hammer and nails. Get with the program, Dutch 'the Toolman' Merrill. Give that old-TV-show guy a run for his money."

"More power, huh?"

I faked a punch to his shoulder. "There you go! Chalk one up for the Toolman."

We all laughed, more out of relief at the averted stand-

off than at my lame excuse for a joke. Then my cell phone
rang.

It was the shipping company about the delayed Guatemalan chairs. A multitude of apologies and excuses followed. I controlled my irritation—what else could I do?
These minor headaches are part and parcel of my much-
loved career.

"So what's the verdict?" Tedd asked.

"Another few days—he *promises*. I was afraid he was
even going to offer me his firstborn kid as collateral for
the chairs."

"That's too bad," Tedd said. "I can't wait to see them.
The samples I fell in love with that time I went to Tijuana
were incredible. I know they're going to look fantastic in
my waiting room."

I grimaced. "So do I . . . if they ever get here."

"Just so long as your part of this deal doesn't slow my
part down," Dutch offered.

"Give me a break! They're just chairs. They go in last,
after you're done doing your thing."

"Come on, kiddies," Tedd said. "Let's try to get along
now—"

"Teddie!" a warbly female voice called from the waiting
room. "Are you here, dear?"

The psychologist glanced at her watch on her way to the
front. "Look at the time! Yes, Darlene. I'm here. Is Jacob
with you?"

"Of course, dear. I wouldn't come without him—it's
Cissy's day off, remember?"

My curiosity got the better of me—when doesn't it? Since we began the redesign of Tedd's office, I'd met more than a few of her other clients. I say "other" because I'm on the books too. Tedd has helped me deal with personal bogeymen a time or two. So I wanted to get a look at Darlene and Jacob, whoever they were.

Besides, something about the elderly woman's voice tugged at me, so I followed Tedd into the waiting room. When I walked past Dutch, I had to do some more ignoring, since he muttered, "There goes that nose again. Snoop, snoop, snoop . . ."

It wasn't easy, but I prevailed. Actually, it was my curiosity that won; it dragged me into the waiting room to catch a glimpse of Darlene and Jacob. I let my dignity squawk.

In the large, boring beige space stood a tall, slender woman who brought to mind lace and tea parties and all the niceties of the late Victorian period. She wore her snow white hair pulled into a soft Gibson-girl knot at the top of her head, and the lapels of her pale mauve silk suit were embellished with tiny seed pearls. A spectacular strand of more pearls, golden and marble sized, circled her neck, while the diamonds on her hands sparkled in the weak incandescent light of the table lamps.

At her side a gentleman stood tall and strong, his hair a steely gray, his eyes almost the same color. But something about his gaze struck me as odd. Sadness swept over me, even though I had no idea why.

"Jacob darling," Darlene said with a pat to one of the

overstuffed beige sofas. "Come sit here while I talk with Teddie. You'll be in the sun, and you know you like that."

The haunting gray eyes turned to Darlene, then to Tedd, to me, and finally back to Darlene. A frown creased Jacob's high forehead.

"Who . . . who are you?"

My stomach sank to my toes. His disorientation spoke loud and clear. Dementia, possibly Alzheimer's. How terribly sad.

With infinite patience Darlene murmured more soothing words. Tedd waited at their side, silent, a soft smile on her lips. I stepped back so as not to disturb Jacob any further.

I prayed under my breath. I asked for strength for Darlene, clarity for Jacob, wisdom for Tedd.

A tear slid down my cheek.

Dutch's large, warm hand settled on my shoulder, and I surprised myself when I leaned back.

"Tough, isn't it?" he whispered.

"I can't begin to imagine."

Darlene took a magazine from the central coffee table, opened it to a colorful ad, and placed it in Jacob's hands.

I glanced at my erstwhile nemesis. "Awesome, isn't she?"

He gave me a crooked grin. "I don't think I could ever come up with that much patience."

"And love . . ."

"For better or for worse . . ."

We watched for long moments until Willa, Tedd's new secretary, stepped out from behind her reception desk and sat next to Jacob. With gentle words she struck up a one-sided conversation with the elderly man.

Only then did Darlene turn to Tedd. "He's had a bad week."

"And you?" Tedd asked.

Darlene shrugged. That's when I noticed that her suit dwarfed her. Either she'd borrowed the outfit, which I doubted, since it seemed so perfect for her, or she'd lost weight—a great deal of weight—since she'd bought it.

Her sigh was more sob than sigh. "I start treatment again next week."

Tedd tried to hide her reaction to Darlene's words, but I'd come to know her pretty well in the last year. The tiny flare of nostrils and the quick blink revealed her shock.

She only nodded. "Want to come in now?"

Darlene stepped into Tedd's counseling office, her shoulders high, her step firm, her demeanor made more tragic by the display of courage.

Before the door closed, Tedd asked, "How many chemo sessions will you need this time?"

I looked up at Dutch.

He looked down at me. "The doors are no big deal."

2

After that it was hard to find fault with Dutch or to hassle over details; I'd just had a look at the greater scheme of things. My troubles were nothing compared to the burden Darlene carried.

I focused on the paint technique I'd chosen for the office walls. For that certain south-of-the-border flavor, without going touristy Mexican, I'd decided on a plaster and glaze finish that would—I hoped—make the plain old drywall look like aged adobe. By the time I'd coated a couple of feet of wall in the tinted goop, I wore almost as much of it as the drywall itself did.

"That is fascinating," Darlene said.

"Ack!" I spun around, the trowel full of glop in hand, and dropped a big splat of the stuff at her feet. "I didn't hear you."

She smiled, although the smile didn't quite make it to her Liz Taylor violet eyes. "I knew Teddie was having work done to the office, and I asked her if I could take a peek. I love what you're doing."

My grin came out crooked. "To the walls or to my clothes?"

Her laugh did brighten her gaze a tad. "It's like I used to tell my boys when they were little—messy, but good."

The globs that clung to the old overalls and tank top I'd brought to change into fit right into the first category. "I've never been accused of being a clean painter, so I guess I shouldn't expect to be a neat faux techniquer either."

"What is that you're using?"

I launched into a detailed explanation, thankful I could give her a short break from the troubles she faced. Her interest fueled my zeal, so I told her how I'd mixed pigment into the mush and would later apply a blend of more color and glaze medium. My goal was a warm, aged hue on the now imperfect texture of the walls.

"I'm so impressed," she said in a sincere voice. "I never would have thought someone might want to make a new place look like . . . well, like my place."

"Really? What's your home like?"

"I guess it's what's called a painted lady, a big, old Victorian with the multicolored gingerbread trim outside and the interior plasterwork they used to do back then. The moldings are dark—Daddy never did let Mama paint them white, no matter how often she told him it looked much too old-fashioned."

I drew a sharp breath. "You didn't paint them, did you?"

She patted my shoulder. "Don't worry, dear. I couldn't bring myself to do it, since Daddy was so opposed. I'm afraid I was a bit of a Daddy's girl."

That breath exploded out in relief. "I'm so glad. It's a crime what some people do to those magnificent old homes. They don't pay attention to the exquisite craftsmanship, the fine materials, the artistry that went into the construction and finish work, the pride the workmen took in everything they did."

"Go, Haley, go!" Dutch cheered.

I turned toward him. "What rock did you crawl out from under? I thought you went to pick up the beams for the ceiling."

"That didn't take long."

I faced Darlene again. "Just ignore him. He's a necessary evil—good for construction and the occasional headache."

Dutch shot me one of his most wicked smiles and waggled a finger under my nose. "Ah-ah-ah! Don't forget, you once saved me from a fate worse than death. That old cliché says now you own me."

"Don't remind me." I wouldn't remind him of the times he'd saved me. The memories weren't good ones, even though I was glad he hadn't been locked up for a murder he didn't commit. "Besides, I gave you back your sorry self. Right away too. You're all your own."

He clutched his clasped hands to his chest. "You wound me, oh, Faux Finished One." He winked at Darlene, who was, inexplicably, charmed by the goofball. "Even though she sure doesn't look like she'll be *finished* here anytime soon."

"Punny, punny. Just not very funny." I tipped up my chin. "You can't rush perfection, Merrill."

"What's with the sloth's pace, Farrell?"

"Oh!" Darlene exclaimed. "Then you're not married."

I squeaked in horror.

Dutch gaped.

Tedd laughed. "You'd think, wouldn't you?"

I spun to face her. "Are you out of your mind? I'd never—"

"Never say never," she cut in. "How's it going out here? That is, besides your usual head butting."

Dutch snorted. "She's slow."

I reached for Darlene's arm, then thought better of putting my plastered paw on that yummy mauve silk. "If we ignore him, he might go away," I said. "It's going well, but you can't hurry the process. It takes layers upon layers to make plain old drywall look like ancient adobe."

"It would seem very well worth the time investment," Darlene said. "The texture she's applied, even though the color is a bit bright, looks like that of the walls in my house. I'd let her go at her pace."

I beamed. "See? A woman of discerning taste."

Darlene again patted my shoulder—carefully, since I had splotches of plaster there too. "And you're a talented young woman. I just might get inspired now that I've seen your work."

"That," Tedd said, "is a wonderful idea. You could use some fun right about now, Darlene. And redecorating, although a pain at times, is fun."

A sigh brought the sadness back to Darlene's violet eyes. "You're right, dear. I haven't had much fun in a long, long time."

The resignation in her voice touched me. "Please let me know if there's anything I can do to help. I love what I do, and I can . . . oh, I don't know. Maybe I can make the process easier for you—with the house, of course. I'm itching to get my hands on a Victorian treasure like yours. You'd be doing me a favor."

Darlene was taken aback. "Oh, no . . . Haley, is it?"

At my nod, she continued. "I can certainly afford a designer, and I insist on paying for your time. You're very young, Haley, and I'm sure just starting out. You can't afford to give away your talent and training like that. Why, you'd wind up in the poorhouse in no time at all."

I blushed.

Tedd chuckled.

Dutch laughed.

When his laughter died down to a few chortles, Dutch said, "Not her. Haley here can probably buy all three of us out and have enough left over to make a nice dent in the national debt. She's a bona-fide filthy-rich heiress."

"I am well off," I said. "But my money came after a tragedy. I was the beneficiary of a friend's will. She died a horrible death. I'd much, much rather still have her around."

"I see." Darlene's voice revealed leashed curiosity. I admired her control—I would've blurted out something stupid and nosy.

An awkward silence swamped us, and the drier-by-the-minute plaster on my trowel didn't fascinate me, but it was the most convenient thing on which to focus.

Once again Darlene displayed her grace and manners.

"This has been lovely, and we'll have to see what I decide about the house. But now I must go rescue dear Willa. It's terribly difficult to keep Jacob calm and entertained for this long. And Teddie dear? If you're smart, you'll make certain you never lose that girl as an employee. She's pure platinum."

Tedd followed Darlene to the front. "She's almost done with her doctorate in psychology, and I've asked her to join my practice, with a partnership in the future, as soon as the ink dries on her state license."

"That little bitty girl . . . ?"

As soon as we were alone, I rounded on Dutch. "You're never going to let me live down my most embarrassing investigative moments, are you?"

He crossed his arms. "How about you? You keep bringing up that old lawsuit—which I won, if you'll remember."

"Hey, a girl's got to keep some kind of leverage around you."

"And a guy's got to watch his step around you. You're danger on wheels."

"Don't you even think of bringing up the dead bodies stuff. Bella's a ghoul and does it all the time. Especially now that she's got herself a PI license."

That set him off again. "Oh . . ." He tried again between laughs. "Oh man. I can just see the two of you now. Haley and the corpses, and Bella and the cats. Ever think of writing a TV script?"

I rolled my eyes. "You're repulsive. Murder is a hideous sin, and here you're turning it into a joke."

"Not the murders, Haley," he said in a soft and serious voice. "Never the deaths or the crimes that caused them." Then he shrugged. "But let's face it. The idea of you skulking through slime-filled trash sheds—" he held up a hand to stop my righteous objection—"which you've been known to do on occasion. And then, just outside the shed, voilà! Bella and her Balis as backup. Look out, Wilmont, Seattle, and all points beyond! Loony ladies on the loose."

I planted my fists on my hips. The trowel splotched plaster down at my feet. "I'll have you know, I am no longer in the corpse-finding business, and Bella has decided to specialize."

He arched a brow. "Oh really? And just what would Bella's specialty be?"

I'd walked right into that one. How was I going to tell him with a straight face? I gave it my best shot. "She's Wilmont's first official pet detective."

This time he laughed so hard that tears poured from his green eyes down his tan cheeks.

In this kind of situation, a girl has just one option.

I joined him.

Three days and one gorgeously faux adobed hall later—well, it still needed a couple more coats of glaze—I had to put in an appearance at Norwalk & Farrell's Auctions. I do own the place. Well, not all of it. My assistant's position was short-lived; I offered Ozzie Krieger a full partnership a couple of days after my inheritance cleared probate.

That he would accept only 40 percent is a consequence

of his faintly tainted past, one we've both agreed to keep where it belongs—in the past.

I walked into our warehouse to hear the scary scrape of wood against cement. "Hey, Ozzie! Are you damaging the merchandise again?"

A short, slender brown tornado spun into my path, his somewhat protuberant eyes open wide. "Oh, my heavens, Miss Haley! I have never damaged one of our pieces. I would never do such a thing. Why, I even have my surgical gloves on."

My brilliant, master-worrywart partner stopped wringing his hands long enough to show me that, yes, he did indeed have on a pair of latex surgical gloves.

"Good grief, Ozzie! What are those for?"

"Well, miss. It's all about the oils on one's fingers. They can mar the integrity of many of the antiques we handle. These pieces are such magnificent exemplars of our historical wealth that I feel honor bound to treat them with the kind of respect pieces of such longevity have earned."

Oh yeah. Ozzie is a fuddy-duddy, and long-winded as a politician. But he knows his antiques. He's a walking, talking encyclopedia of styles, availability, details of provenance, value, and probable selling price too. He refuses to drop the *Miss* in front of my name. When he refused the 50 percent ownership I offered him in favor of the 40, that left me the senior partner, and even though he's old enough to be my very young grandfather and is more knowledgeable and experienced than I ever hope to be, he feels he must defer to my position.

I wish he'd taken the stupid 50 percent.

"I heard you moving furniture," I went on. "That usually has some kind of finish on it, and the oils on your fingers won't hurt it a whole lot."

The slim man practically quivered with excitement. "Ah! But you see, Miss Haley, I have found a treasure in the Pennsylvania highboy we acquired last month. Evidently, its former owner didn't realize a treasure hid behind one of the drawers. I found a *fraktur* pen-and-ink piece!"

I may know my furniture styles, but many other antiques still mystify me. "What's a *fraktur*?"

You'd a thunk I'd smacked him one by the look of horror he put on. "Miss Haley! You must know what Pennsylvania Dutch *frakturs* are."

I counted to ten. "No, Ozzie. I don't know what Pennsylvania Dutch *frakturs* are. Remember, I'm an interior designer, not an art historian, museum curator, or antiques expert. That's your job around here."

He *ahemed* and squared his shoulders. "Well, miss. Strictly speaking, a *fraktur* is an ornate type of written or printed German, similar to Gothic lettering in English. Pennsylvania Dutch *Geburts und Taufscheine*—that's birth and baptismal certificates, you know—and other such kind of documents often employed *fraktur* lettering. Nowadays the documents themselves are called *frakturs*, even when they have no *fraktur* lettering at all. Most of the time they are decorated with magnificent pen-and-ink drawings of stylized birds and flowers and cherubs—"

"Oh, yeah, yeah. *Frakturs*. Thanks, Ozzie. Now I know all about them."

What can I say? I had to stop him. He would've gone on and on—with no break—for the next month describing his favorite *frakturs*; who was responsible for them; where he'd seen, bought, and sold them—and to whom—and who the original birthday boy or girl had been.

He looked at me as though I'd grown another head. "I doubt you can know everything about them, Miss Haley—"

"That's what I keep you around for, Ozzie. You're the one who knows all that important stuff—*information*. So. I guess this *fraktur* is pretty special, then."

"We rarely see any on the West Coast. Collectors in the east snap them up the moment they become available. And this one's a good one, from the heart of Pennsylvania Dutch country, dated 1840."

"And you found it stuck in the highboy?"

"To the back and underneath a drawer, Miss Haley. You can't begin to imagine my exhilaration when I found the piece. And it is in museum condition."

"But why were you moving furniture?"

His eyes bugged out even more, and red tinted his balding pate. "In my enthusiasm, I . . . ah . . . dropped it, miss. And I must retrieve it from under the highboy before it is damaged due to my careless negligence."

"Oh, give it up, Ozzie. You've never been careless or negligent. Let me help you so we can get the piece back in your well-protected fingers again."

Moments later I came face-to-face with my first real, live Pennsylvania Dutch *fraktur*. I fell in love. The piece was indeed stylized, the birds and tulips on the page similar to those on old barn hex signs. I went to my office, my head jam-packed with questions about the child the document honored . . . Fritz Gerhardt, born August 16, 1840.

The phone rang and put an end to my mental time travel. "Norwalk & Farrell Auctions, Haley Farrell speaking."

There was a pause. Then, "Haley? It's Darlene Weikert. Tedd Rodriguez's client. I don't know if you remember me—"

"Of course I remember you. Have you seen the walls?"

"Yes, dear. I saw them when I went to my appointment yesterday. And they're in part the reason I called you."

My heartbeat kicked it up a notch. "Really?"

"I mentioned to you the other day that I might want to update parts of the family home, and Tedd insisted it would be fun. I've decided to go ahead and do something about the parlor and dining room, since those are the rooms that seem most stuck in the past."

"Now, you don't expect me to do anything to the Victorian integrity of the home, do you?"

"No, not really. But Mama's wallpaper is so faded you can't see the roses very well, and the woodwork is nicked and scratched in places. What I'd like to do is restore the home rather than redecorate it."

Be still my heart! "And you called me because . . . ?"

"Because you were so passionate about the workmanship."

I heard her smile in her words. I bet she remembered Dutch's goofy cheer. "Are you asking me to . . . ?"

"I'm being very clumsy, dear. What I'd like is to hire your services for the restoration."

Oh yeah! "I'm honored, Mrs. Weikert. Of course, I'd love to work with you."

"Please call me Darlene. It'll make working together that much more pleasant."

"I can't wait, Darlene. When would you like to start?"

I heard the ruffle of pages as she checked either a calendar or a date book. "How does Thursday sound?"

"Excellent." I fought to keep the impatience out of my voice.

"Will four o'clock work? That's Jacob's usual nap time."

"How is he this week?"

She sighed. "He's never really well, but he's had a less difficult week than the last few."

"I'm glad to hear that, for your sake as well as his." I wondered if I should ask after her health, but I decided that for once I'd dredge up some tact.

"Then it's a date," Darlene said. "I'll see you Thursday afternoon."

"Thank you so much for your trust. I won't let you down."

"Of course you won't, dear. You're a very, very gifted young woman."

I launched the countdown—days, hours, seconds—after I hung up.

It was a too-long week. By the time Thursday finally got around to showing up, I was as ready to roar as an orbital sander on a fresh-milled board.

I got to the Weikerts' gorgeous Queen Anne Victorian five minutes early. What can I say? I am impatient. Then I sat in my Honda and salivated until it was time to slip to the other side of the ornamental wrought-iron gate in the decorative fence, climb the porch steps, grab the brass doorknocker, and put it to use.

While I waited for someone to come to the door after I knocked, I turned around to admire the original ginger-bread trim along the roofline of the wide, graceful porch.

"Who're you?"

I spun at Jacob Weikert's question.

"Jacob?"

"No, you're not Jacob. I'm Jacob. Who're you?"

He should have been in bed. "Ah . . . I'm here to see Darlene."

"Darlene . . . ?" He glanced over his shoulder. Then he looked out to the street. "Darlene who?"

A tiny woman, maybe all of five feet tall, rushed up be-hind the befuddled man. "You're supposed to be resting, Jacob. What are you doing down here?"

"Well, I heard a ring . . ."

She tsk-tsked and took his arm. "That's no reason to get up. I can take care of the door. Let's go up to your room again, okay?"

He frowned, scratched his head. "Where's my room? I don't remember."

"I'll help you." As she led Jacob across the foyer, she called out. "You must be Haley. I'm Cissy Grover. Darlene's expecting you. I'll let her know you're here."

I stood in the doorway, unsure of what to do. I could always do my usual and barge right in. The aged mahogany woodwork around the two doorways that led off the foyer was calling my name. And the leaded glass window at the stair landing begged me to go check it out.

But this wasn't my house. And I hadn't been invited inside.

True, Darlene had hired me to restore the parlor and dining room, but she hadn't come down yet, and with the memory of her exquisite manners fresh in my mind, I decided not to do anything to put her off.

I heard Cissy call Darlene upstairs. I waited for the response but heard nothing.

"Darlene honey," she said again. "Your designer's here."

The same.

I couldn't have gotten the day mixed up—Cissy had said Darlene was expecting me.

As the minutes ticked by with no response from my new client, uneasiness lurked around my gut. Something wasn't right here.

A little voice in the back of my mind screamed, "Go!" but I chose to ignore it. I wanted the job.

More time trickled by.

With every beat of my heart, my anxiety grew.

Then, "Oh no! Darlene! Please wake up. Please, honey. Please!"

The little voice morphed into a table saw's roar. But by then I couldn't take a single step. Memories battered me. Icy chills racked me. I stood frozen in place.

As if from a great distance, I heard Cissy run partway down the grand staircase. "Please call an ambulance. I can't wake Darlene—she's not breathing. I think . . . I'm afraid . . . oh, Haley, hurry, hurry, hurry! I think Darlene's dead."

I still couldn't move. *No, no, no, no, no, no, no. This can't be.*

"What am I saying?" Cissy wailed. "She's dead. I don't want her to be dead, but she is. No pulse . . . no breath . . . cold. She's dead."

I dragged myself out of my numb state, reached in my backpack purse for my cell phone, and hit a number that was altogether too familiar by now.

Don't ask me why.

It's a long story I don't like to rehash.

But I didn't call the ambulance just then. I called the Wilmont PD instead.

3

Wilmont PD Homicide Detective Lila Tsu and I have met a number of times, but never under pleasant circumstances. This time was no different.

The moment she drove up in her plain-vanilla four-door sedan, she stabbed me with that razor-sharp stare of hers. "I should have known you'd be here."

"Why would you say that?"

"Let's see here." She began to tick off fingers. "We have a big, old house in Wilmont, Washington. We have an interior designer. And we also have a dead woman on the premises. In my experience, that adds up to Haley Farrell."

"That's so not fair, Lila. I didn't find the body. As a matter of fact, I haven't even seen it. I've yet to set foot inside the house."

The elegant detective pulled her trademark silver pen and a notepad from her chic black handbag. "Who is the victim?"

I frowned. "You know, I'm not sure she *is* a victim. At least, not of anything more than some form of cancer."

"Do you mean to tell me there's been no crime? And you called me?"

Swallow me, earth. "Ah . . . maybe."

"Why? Why would you call me?"

"I . . . I can't really say. Maybe it was a knee-jerk reaction. You know—the big, old house, the dead female, and the designer." The only thing missing was Dutch, but I wasn't about to mention him.

She tucked her notepad and pen back into her bag. "You're certifiable. But while I'm here, I guess it doesn't hurt to check things out."

Lila's shoes rapped sharply on the aged floor. My knees decided to quit on me, and I collapsed on the top porch step. How could this happen again? And to me?

I turned to prayer. And while I leaned on my reemerging faith, the shivers and shudders never stopped. I'd really wanted to work with Darlene. I hardly knew her, but I did know I'd met a woman of enviable character who didn't hesitate to show the depth of her love. I felt cheated by her death.

Darlene hadn't met with foul play, had she?

After a while the front door opened again. "I'm happy to report," Lila said, "Mrs. Weikert appears to have died in her sleep. Their live-in nurse, Mrs. Grover, told me about the recurrence of the liver cancer. There's not much doubt as to the cause of death, Haley. You can relax."

"That doesn't make it a whole lot better, does it?"

"I understand."

We didn't talk for a bit. Then Lila broke the silence. "Just so you know. We're now related in a strange kind of way. We've been adopted by brothers."

A spark of humor caught fire. "Woo-hoo! You sure took your time. How's the pup?"

"He's terrific—and a terror! But then they all are."

"That means you don't spend every waking minute at the cop shop anymore."

"No, Haley. I don't spend every waking minute at the department these days. But I do have to get back. There's nothing here for me."

"Can't say I'm sorry to see you go."

"I'll give you that. Will I see you at Tyler's *dojo* anytime soon?"

"I'm there every Thursday night. How about you?"

"I still teach the Wednesday morning lesson. It doesn't look as if our paths will cross."

"Well, then, take care."

"You too."

Weird. I wasn't thrilled to see her go. As Tyler Colby, our *sensei*, once said, the detective and I have more than a few things in common. And even though she tried her best to pin a murder on me when we first met, I've since come to respect her determination and her devotion to her job.

She's also a killer sparring partner.

And speaking of sparring, two men made their way up the walk toward me, their faces red, their voices raised, their pace fast and furious. Both punctuated their arguments with jabs and stabs of raised arms.

"You don't know what you're talking about, Tommy,"

the one on the left said. "Mother knows about your dirty little secret."

"What dirty little secret? I have nothing to hide."

From the sideways shift of his murky blue eyes, I'd bet he had more than a thing or two to hide.

"What secret?" not-Tommy bellowed. "Hey, I know how you tinker with the odometers down at that dealership of yours—"

"Those are fighting words, Larry. I take my business very seriously, and all a businessman has is his integrity."

Larry hooted.

Tommy sputtered.

I cringed. Who were these two?

"Hey!" Larry called out. "Who're you?"

Since I was alone on the porch, they must've meant me. "Ah . . . the interior designer."

That stopped them.

Wow! What power.

I took advantage of their stunned silence. "And who might you two be?"

"I'm Larry Weikert, and this clown's my younger brother, Tommy. But we don't need an overpriced decorator."

These were Darlene's sons? Darlene, the genteel Victorian, raised these two?

You'd think some of her dignity would've rubbed off—at the very least some of her sense of style should've trickled down.

But no. Tommy wore a sleazy, mega-slick emerald silk shirt—untucked—and a snazzy pair of skin-tight pinstriped dark denim jeans. His loafers looked butter soft, and I suspected they started life in a custom footwear designer's atelier in Italy. Larry, on the other hand, had on the stereotypical computer nerd's uniform—a faded T-shirt embellished with code gobbledygook, ratty jeans, and sneakers with vent holes at the toe. A plastic protector full of pens poked out from the T's puny pocket.

"Did Cissy call you?" I asked. They didn't look like grief-stricken offspring.

"Cissy?" Larry asked. "Nah. She's too busy keeping dear old Dad out of trouble."

I stood, afraid the ugly job of breaking the news sat square on my shoulders. "Then you don't know yet."

Larry's glasses wiggled on his long nose. "Know what?"

"I have bad news." It wasn't going to be easy no matter how I worded it, and before I could stop myself, I blurted out, "Your mother's dead."

"Huh?"

"What?"

"You'd better go in. Cissy can tell you more. But I can tell you your mother passed away sometime this afternoon."

Tommy went primer white.

Larry blinked behind his bottle-bottom lenses.

I'd botched it, so I scrambled for alternatives, fell back on years of training, and used my best preacher's daughter's voice. "I'm so sorry for your loss. But come on. Come on inside. Cissy's going to need help with the decisions that must be made."

The sons came onto the porch like a pair of zombies. They

stared at the door, which was still ajar, each step they took slower than the last. On their way in, Tommy muttered something about bankruptcy and jail time.

My heart ached for Darlene. What these two must have put her through . . . But now she was beyond pain. I wondered about her faith. I hoped she'd placed it in the Lord.

I almost made it to my Honda.

"Haley!" Cissy called from the porch. "Hold on a minute, please."

The petite woman hurried down the steps, past the iron-grill gate in the fence, and across the small lawn to where I'd parked in the driveway. Grief ravaged her plain features; tears poured from her swollen eyes.

She held out her right hand. "I'm glad to finally meet you."

Her fingers were ice cold. "Really?"

"For days Darlene talked about little else but what you're doing at Dr. Rodriguez's office and how much she wanted to hear your ideas for her family home."

"I see."

"No, I don't think you do." A sob shook her, but she closed her eyes, then stood tall and firm. "The last few years have been a day-to-day nightmare for Darlene. She watched the man she loved descend into an ever-thicker fog, and the liver cancer she battled and believed she'd beaten returned. Then the boys . . . well, she never could count on them for anything."

I sensed her need to speak, to release some pain, so I murmured a vague "hmm . . ."

"She did listen when the oncologist urged her to seek counseling. For a while the depression went so deep that I . . . I thought it would take her rather than the cancer."

She glanced at the house and sighed. "I can't believe she's gone. Especially now. She was doing so much better. She was ready to fight the malignancy, and her spirits . . . well, you know? It's been years since I've seen her as excited as she was about working with you. She loves—loved—this house."

My throat knotted up. *Why, Lord? Why now?*

We studied Darlene's home, each consumed by private thoughts. Then, down the street, a car horn honked. I dragged in a gulp of air, and Cissy shook her head.

"Oh, would you just look at me?" She wiped her eyes with shaky fingers. "I didn't want to believe it, but somewhere inside I knew it was just a matter of time. Now that it's happened, I've turned into a blubbery old woman. And I'm holding you back. I'm sure you have better things to do than listen to a silly old fool bawl over something that can't be changed."

"Oh, no! Please don't think that. I only met Darlene that one time, but she made a huge impression on me. I doubt anyone could've met her and not admired her. I wanted to work with her, and I'm so sad I won't have the chance to know her better."

It must've been what Cissy needed to hear. She gave me a watery smile. "Everyone loves—loved—her. Even the nurses and lab techs at the doctor's office, and they don't speak much English."

"That's strange. I've never heard that the Fred Hutchinson Cancer Institute staffs that many non-English speakers."

Cissy bit her bottom lip. She glanced again at the house, then shrugged. "I guess I don't need to keep her secret any longer. Darlene supplemented her standard chemo from the oncologist at the institute with HGH—human growth hormone. She believed, as lots of researchers do, that it's the key to healing and longevity."

"Human growth hormone? I don't know a whole lot about the stuff. I did skim through a couple of stories in the paper about it coming in from Mexico, but that was a while ago."

"Darlene didn't use smuggled serum—that's dangerous. We went down to Dr. Díaz, a specialist in HGH therapy, just over the border in Tijuana. He'd sell us a six-week supply, and I'd inject her here at home."

"She really thought it would work?"

Cissy squared her shoulders. "You have to look at the research before you can make up your mind. I came to my own conclusions after I read a large number of clinical studies."

"I suppose you agree with Darlene—and that Dr. Díaz."

"There's a lot to HGH therapy. And after only five months, Darlene began to improve daily. That's why her death comes as such a blow. She'd even gained some weight."

"But I heard her say she had to start chemo again."

Cissy sniffed. "I think the orthodox medical community has too great an interest in boosting the sale of chemo drugs. They keep patients scared almost to death by a cancer diagnosis. But most of those doctors own stock in drug companies. I'm not sure Darlene had relapsed. Besides, the so-called legit guys don't bother to tell anyone there's hope elsewhere."

"Okay." Fanatics come in all flavors.

"And what's more, those of us who have looked into it are certain there's more potential for HGH than even as a cure for cancer. We believe it's the real fountain of youth. Sooner or later a researcher's going to unravel its secret and provide humanity with eternal life."

Visions of *The Twilight Zone* danced in my head. Time to split. "Well, Cissy. That's very interesting, of course, but you're right. I do have to hurry back to work."

The look on her face said she had my number. "Don't forget," she added. "Everyone thought the world was flat once too."

Oh boy. "That's a good point, and I'll give it some more thought. But I gotta go." I opened the car door and slipped in behind the wheel. "Please let me know if there's anything I can do to help."

Her inner fire fizzled out. "There's not much anyone can do. Darlene's dead."

And that was that.

Or so I thought.

At dinner that night, Dad seemed quieter than usual. "What's on your mind?" I asked.

He put down his fork. "I know I'm absentminded, but I've never forgotten a church member before."

"What makes you think you have now?"

"I had an odd call right before I left the office. It delayed me a little."

"I wondered."

"It was the strangest thing, Haley. A young man called to ask me to perform his mother's funeral, said she spoke highly of my sermons. But I don't know him, and I can't remember her either."

"Maybe something kept her from coming the last few years, and she's slipped your mind."

"Then she must have slipped our roster too. I couldn't find record of her membership, tithing, or even a random donation over the last eight years. And I do take those matters seriously."

Dad obsesses about the accuracy of the church's finances.

"That is strange," I said. "But maybe the son was mistaken. Maybe she attended a different church."

"I thought of that, so I called him back. And that call's what made me late. He insisted ours is the one, said she used to walk to services, that it has to be the Wilmont River Church because there's none other that close to the home."

"So what are you going to do?"

"Well, I suppose I'll perform the service, even though I don't feel right about it. I mean . . . I don't know the woman, and I hate to deliver a generic, meaningless message."

I reached across the table to pat his hand. "Don't worry, Dad. You could never give a meaningless sermon. You have a way of teaching God's Word that reaches at least one little corner of your listeners' hearts."

"Seems to me you spent years with all those little corners of your heart closed to my preaching."

"Yes, but if you'll remember, I had to stay away to do it."

"So that's why you participated in the congregation's activities but avoided Sunday services."

"It was the only way I could stay angry with God."

He lowered his gaze, and I knew it wasn't the remains of his meatloaf and mashed potatoes that had him in thrall. When he looked up again, I saw the moisture in his eyes.

"I'm very thankful you've come back, Haley."

"So am I, Dad. So am I."

I took our plates to the dishwasher, then gathered bowls, spoons, mugs, the coffeepot, and a carton of mocha chip ice cream. By the time I plunked it all on the table, my mouth watered in anticipation of my favorite ice cream.

"I see you stopped by the store," Dad said with a grin. "No strawberry?"

"Hey! You know the rules. He—or she—who buys gets to choose. Got a problem with that rule, Daddy-o?" I winked. "Oh, that's right. You can't have a problem with it—you're the one who made it!"

"Dish it up, honey. Just dish it up."

After the first spoonful or ten of frozen bliss, I returned to our earlier topic. "Hey, you never told me the name of the woman. I might remember her. You never know what kind of fuzz might stick to my mental Velcro."

"It's Darlene Weikert—"

The clatter of the spoon against my ice cream bowl cut off whatever else Dad might have said. My shock painted a frown on his face.

"Haley? Are you all right?"

"No way are you going to believe this," I said after a handful of deep, measured breaths. "Recently Darlene asked me to do her parlor and dining room. We had an appointment for this afternoon, but when I got there—"

"Oh no. Haley! Not again."

"What can I say? I got there at four like we'd agreed, and their live-in nurse—Mr. Weikert has what I think is Alzheimer's—went to tell her I was there. Cissy, the nurse, couldn't wake Darlene, and she started to yell, asked me to get an ambulance. The rest is history."

He closed his eyes in what I knew from experience was silent prayer. Then, "How was this poor woman murdered?"

"Good grief, Dad! Not you too!"

"What do you mean, not you too?"

I blew a curl off my left eyebrow. "The minute she showed up, Lila Tsu started up with this totally bogus 'old house in Wilmont plus interior designer plus dead female equals Haley Farrell' deal."

"You have to admit you have a strong track record."

"Not! But guess what? Nobody killed Darlene. She had cancer."

His relief mirrored mine of this afternoon—but I operate on a need-to-know basis, and he didn't need to know that.

"There's one bit of good news," he said.

"Yepper. So what did you tell the son? Oh, and which one called? Tommy or Larry?"

"You know her children? My goodness, Haley! You've become another Bella."

I took a boxer's stance. "Wanna go a round or two, Rev?"

He grinned. "You're the one who says Bella knows everyone. Now it turns out you know this woman, and even her sons. That sounds a lot like Bella Cahill."

"Okay. Scratch that. Forget I mentioned the younger Weikerts. What'd you say to the son who called?"

"I told him I'd officiate, but only if he could give me a list of her favorite hymns and a couple of Scripture verses that meant something to her."

The Tommy and Larry I'd met didn't seem as if they'd know how to track down hymns or verses.

"What did he say to that?"

"Oh, he took his time, hemmed and hawed, but I wouldn't agree until he accepted my conditions. I have to know something about the woman's faith."

"Don't be surprised if you get a list with stuff like 'Hymn for the Cyberwhiz' and quotes from *The Slimy Auto Salesman's Bible*."

He narrowed his eyes. "You do know Mrs. Weikert's sons."

"More than I want to."

"When did you meet them?"

"This afternoon."

"And you've already formed a negative opinion of them?" He shook his head. "That's not like you. Why?"

I raised one shoulder. "They showed up at Darlene's house when I was on my way out. They were angry, in the middle of an argument about Tommy's business ethics—or lack thereof—and seemed only surprised to hear their mother had died. Neither one looked particularly sad at the news."

"It was probably the shock of the moment, honey."

"She'd fought liver cancer for years, Dad. I don't know how much shock comes with that kind of death."

He still looked doubtful.

"Tell you what," I offered. "When will you meet with them?"

"Tomorrow afternoon."

"Let's compare notes at dinner. Give me your take then."

"You have yourself a deal."

And with that, I put the Weikert family out of my mind. I had a Latina shrink's office to south-of-the-borderize.

By two o'clock the next day, my curiosity made it impossible to pin another curtain or sew another cushion for Tedd's office. I had to know how the Weikert brothers showed up at the church. I also wanted to see Dad's reaction when they did.

Since I usually sew at home rather than on-site, it was no

big deal to pop into the church and find the time for Dad's appointment—he posts his schedule on a blackboard by his office door. So by three fifteen I'd made myself comfortable with a book on color choices for the new millennium in a pew with a straight shot at Dad's office. I settled in to wait for the grieving siblings.

If I'd really wanted to see them, I would've had to wait nigh unto forever. They didn't show. It was Cissy who came to meet with Dad. I heard her murmured excuses for the brothers—work for Tommy and a broken-down car for Larry.

When Dad ushered Cissy inside, I got the worst itch to go listen at the door. To my credit, I didn't do it. But I did have to scrape up all my willpower to stay put and wait until the meeting was over.

When I saw Cissy emerge from the office and shake Dad's hand, I hurried to get to the church door before she stepped out to the parking lot.

"Cissy!" I cried. "What a surprise. I never expected to see you here." True—I'd expected the brothers. "How's Jacob? How are *you*?"

"This is a surprise, Haley. I came to make arrangements for . . . for Darlene's final farewell." She glanced up at the sky, as if to look for her friend among the clouds. "And Jacob's the same. I'm not sure he's aware of Darlene's passing."

"That's sad, but understandable." The dark circles under her eyes tattled on her. "You haven't slept much, have you?"

She shook her head, and a tear rolled down her cheek.

"She was my closest friend. Yes, I worked for her, but she hired me because we'd been friends for so long. I really miss her."

"I understand. I lost a close friend about a year and a half ago, and I still miss her."

"Please tell me it doesn't hurt this much anymore."

She didn't shake off the arm I wrapped around her shoulders. "The loss is still there." I tried to put into words what had been feelings and sensations too private to expose. "But that hole the death leaves behind . . . it never fills back up. The pain? It's not as sharp anymore. It's kind of . . . like when your hammer smacks your thumb. The first *wham* really hurts, but then it turns . . ."

Cissy gave a weak chuckle. "I understand. Of course, I've lost my parents, my husband, and my daughter . . . my daughter died back in the sixties. Losing Darlene is different. I don't have anyone left."

"My dad and one of our neighbors have said something like that. They use their work to fight the loneliness." If you could call Bella's fads work.

Cissy stepped back, and I didn't try to hold her. "I've tried to do that since yesterday. Work, work, and more work. I had no idea how complex Darlene's business matters would turn out to be."

"You're handling her . . . what? Is it the estate?"

"She named me executrix, if you can believe it. To be honest, I don't understand the half of it. I do know I have to keep those two sons from getting their greedy paws on her funds."

"I don't understand. Don't they inherit her estate?"

"Not at all. Nine years ago they demanded she turn over their trust funds, and she did just that. They went through the money as fast as I expected, and they've mooched off her ever since."

"So if the sons don't inherit, then I suppose she left everything to Jacob—for his care, I'd imagine."

"Something like that." She nodded toward the parking lot. "Walk with me to the car. It's hard to drive it. I can still see Darlene behind the wheel of her brand-new silver baby—that's what she called it. But I still can't get used to all that luxury."

Luxury? Uh-oh. "You were saying about the sons . . . ?"

Cissy nodded. "Darlene loved her sons, but she knew them too. Can you believe she left me the house, her investments—everything—so I can care for Jacob until . . . until . . ."

My mind freaked at all the bizarre input. Flashing red alerts went off. You'd have thought I had an ambulance, complete with siren and spinning lights, way up there.

Suddenly Darlene's death didn't hit me as natural, caused by cancer. Greedy sons cut from the will; a husband lost in the mist of Alzheimer's; a best friend who inherits everything, everything but what it costs to care for the terminally ill widower.

But Darlene *had* suffered from liver cancer.

I couldn't get away from that.

". . . and I even have to meet with the president of the

Wilmont People's Bank tomorrow. Something about the transfer of loan payments into my name."

The word *bank* stuck on my freaked-out mind. "Huh?"

"Oh, more about the estate. It's what Darlene arranged with Roberto Díaz."

"Díaz? Is that the same Díaz who sold her the HGH?"

"The same."

I felt like Alice in my very own, hyperloopy Wonderland. Things grew curiouser and curiouser by the minute. "Loan payments? Darlene owed the doctor for her treatment?"

"Of course not. *She* made *him* a loan so he could buy the lab that manufactures the HGH serum. He's been paying her back on a steady basis. He only has another fifty thousand dollars to go."

I staggered back. Fifty grand! That looked like a whole lot of motive going on. What if . . . ? "Is he current with his payments?"

Cissy averted her gaze. "Oh, Dr. Díaz is a very honorable man, Haley. He has only his patients' best interests at heart. Darlene thought the world of him. She had total faith in his work. And him. Him too."

Those sirens in my head were making me deaf. "I didn't ask you that, Cissy. Did Dr. Díaz fall behind on his payments?"

She tucked her black leather purse tighter under her arm; she smoothed her short, pewter-colored hair over her right ear; she shifted her weight from her right foot to the left. "Um . . ."

"So Darlene's good doctor isn't really all that good."

The new heiress wouldn't face me but instead started

toward the beautiful silver Mercedes, so new that it glowed in the rare Pacific Northwest sunlight—Darlene's new silver baby. Luxury all the way.

Hmm . . .

"Cissy," I said in my sternest voice. "Are you certain Darlene died of cancer?"

Her eyes widened, and she hurried to the car. "I—"

I never heard what she started to say, but I sure wished I had. She pulled into the street with the screech of tires and the roar of a monster German engine.

Billy Shakespeare said it best way back when: something smelled rotten in the state of Denmark . . . Washington.

Whatever.

4

So did I call Lila, or did I check things out first?

The question rumbled in my head the whole night. I tossed and turned with pillows and blankets. But all these thoughts made sleep impossible.

What should I do? It didn't help that Cissy had charmed Dad or that his opinion of the AWOL brothers rivaled mine. I, of course, hadn't repeated my conversation with Cissy.

On the one hand, it seemed everyone but the ailing widower had a reason to want Darlene dead. The brothers were prime candidates for Slime Bucket of the New Millennium, neither one solvent from the look or sound of it. The Mexican doc had fifty grand hanging in the balance. And the poor relation—so to speak—had become an heiress through Darlene's death.

Yeah, yeah, yeah. Been there, done that.

Everyone thought the same when Marge Norwalk, my mentor and friend, died and left me my first savings account with a balance, her auction house, her snazzy home in a gated community that I promptly sold since it was so fancy it made my teeth itchy, and her fat investment portfolio. But I hadn't known a thing about the inheritance until the day after Marge's death. From what Cissy had said that afternoon, my suspicion-o-meter said she knew about Darlene's will from the start.

She just had to wait until Jacob joined his wife. Then she wouldn't have to share the wealth. From where I stood, Jacob Weikert wouldn't be among us much longer.

Would anyone believe me?

Did *I* believe me?

Could Cissy have killed Darlene? She was pretty broken up when she realized she'd never wake her friend again. Could the retired nurse be that good an actress?

I still remembered the icy chill of her fingers when she'd shaken my hand that sad afternoon. Could someone turn down their internal thermometer at will?

Then again, what about the two snarky sons? Either one could have done in their mother. I'm sure that even though they didn't strike me as the shiniest bobeches on the candelabra, they had enough gray matter to realize her illness offered a perfect cover for the crime. Larry had said something about bankruptcy and jail as they'd walked past me on their way in.

Plus the doctor. What kind of guy built a career around the sale of voodoo medicine to desperate, terminally ill senior citizens? And then borrowed buckets of dough from one of them? What part had he played in this tragedy? Was it a tragedy? I mean, beyond the death of a really neat lady.

Or was this a case of my imagination run wild on its own?

Every so often, I'd fall into a light nap. By the time my alarm clock belched out its daily squawk, I'd become an overtired zombie. I couldn't get my head around the idea of motion, had no desire to do more than roll over and try to catch some more of those evasive z's.

But reality was . . . well, real. Dutch and I had an appointment with the guy from the flooring supply place. I had to fake enough brain function to choose the perfect species of wood and then the right shade of stain for Tedd's office floors. And, as always, I had to be ready to do battle with my nemesis, since agreement between us was a rare thing.

Who knows how, but I made it to Tedd's office before Dutch. I'd made myself a bucket of Starbucks House Blend at home, but partway to the meeting, I'd had to make a pit stop for a second, massive infusion of the stuff.

With a sloshy waxed-paper vat in one hand and my trusty portfolio in the other, I collapsed into one of Tedd's comfy if boring office sofas. The flooring guy walked in about three seconds later. The man responsible for the installation of the boards I was about to choose kept us chilling for about another fifteen minutes.

When Dutch finally decided to join us, I gulped down my last swig of caffeine. "What kept you?"

His look doused me with full-strength disgust. "Forget that. I have a question for you, and I think I know the answer already, but I'll ask anyway. Have you read this week's *Wilmont Voice*?"

"Are you kidding? Read the paper? Have you looked at your watch? It's almost the middle of the night! My eyes don't focus until nine o'clock at the earliest."

"I've noticed." He held out a folded issue of our fair hamlet's press offering. "Here. Glug down more java, make your eyes work, and read the front page."

I stuck my index finger in my right ear and gave it a bunch of healthy wiggles. "You know, Dutch. I remember we had this conversation about a year and a half ago. That time I was still in bed and you were on the phone. I could've—and should've—hung up on you and gone back to my blanket and pillow. Unfortunately, I don't have that choice today."

"Go ahead," he urged. "At least look at the headline."

I rolled my eyes. "I guess I'd better humor you—"

The full color photo of Cissy Grover stole my breath away. A gander at the headline nearly did me in. It blared "Nurse/Companion Takes It All."

"Oh-oh-oh-oh-oh-oh—"

"Take the needle off the broken record, Haley. Read on down, will you?"

"What more do I have to know?" I tapped the eyepopper of a headline. "This says it all, doesn't it?"

"Oh, I'm not so sure."

The taunt in his voice fired off all my alarms. But I couldn't stop the freight train known as Dutch Merrill.

"I recognized another name somewhere farther down,"

he said, "somewhere around the middle of the column. Check it out before you say another word."

The sharp edge on his stare set my gut on lurch mode. I'd seen that look before. I didn't like it then, and I liked it no more now. So I did as he asked.

Great. Sure enough, there it was. My name. In black and white. The article placed me at the Weikert home at the time Cissy discovered Darlene's corpse.

He was going to have fun with this one.

I wasn't.

I dragged myself up out of the chair and chose to defend myself with a hearty offense. "What are you up to, Merrill? Are you going to try and pin this murder on me too?"

The unsuspecting floor salesman gasped. Dutch and I turned, glared, then went back to our . . . um . . . discussion.

"Are you guilty?" he asked, even though I knew he knew I wasn't, couldn't be, no way, no how.

"Go pound salt."

"Okay. Sure. But I'm dying to know how you managed to do it—again. Let's see. We have a big, old house. In Wilmont—that's part of the Haley Farrell equation, you know. Of course, there's the interior designer in the picture—that would be you. And just after the *ding-dong* at the door, the housekeeper finds a dead woman upstairs. Sounds familiar, doesn't it?"

"No! No, no, no, no, no, no, *no!*"

"Ahem."

"Tedd!" Had I ever been happier to see someone? Well, maybe Dad when he bailed me out of jail after Dutch and

Lila worked so hard to put me there—unjustly, I might add. But still. "Would you tell this bozo I had nothing to do with Darlene's death?"

"She had nothing to do with Darlene Weikert's death—the woman had liver cancer." She pointed an index finger at each of us. "And you two kiddies need to call a truce. My office! There's a lot to do, and it won't get done while you two squabble. I have missing chairs, unmade curtains, floors that need fixing."

"Cancer?" Dutch asked, ignoring most of what Tedd said, while zooming in on the one word.

My smile reeked of smug. "You didn't read to the end, did you?"

"But there's all that money, the nurse, the sons—*you*!"

"Sorry, Dutch. You can't get rid of me that easy. Get over it. If anyone did something to Darlene, I don't know about it. And I wasn't part of it."

He crossed his arms. "Then I don't have to worry that the interior designer on the job will skip out and take off on another snooping gig."

"Ah . . . no! No, no. Of course not." Did the guy read minds and nightmares by long distance? "Why would you think I'd do such a thing?"

"Because I know you. Your pal Bella and her PI license have nothing on you."

"Haley! Dutch!" Tedd's cheekbones matched the earthy rose timeworn adobe glaze I'd put on her walls. "Time out. My office needs you. You can get back to the merits of Haley's investigative skills later on."

"Or not." With utmost dignity I opened my portfolio and turned to the floor guy. "Mr. Watanabe, here's a sample of the wood from the chairs I ordered for the waiting room. As you can see, they're nearly black, and while I don't want to wind up with matchy-matchy woods, I do want to co-ordinate tones . . ."

Once I got the meeting back on track, it took us no more than fifteen minutes to come to an agreement. For the dis-tressed wide-plank floors, we chose a medium stain that would let the unique chairs shine on their own. Dutch's only objection rose when I insisted on distressed floors—his crew would have to stomp on, hammer, and beat with old chains the fresh boards when they arrived.

"I oppose defacing fine wood on principle," he muttered after Mr. Watanabe left.

I zipped my portfolio. "So oppose it on another job. You'll get it once everything's done. Remember, I'm trying to cre-ate a look here."

He tossed the keys to his decrepit old truck in the air. "So long as you stick to creating a look here rather than looking to create something out there"—he pointed at the paper—"then I guess I'll find a way to be okay with it."

"Suck it up, Dutch." I slung the strap of the leather port-folio over my shoulder. "Darlene had cancer. She asked me to restore her parlor and dining room. That's why I was there. She died of cancer before I had the chance to do the work."

I held my breath. I hadn't lied. Would he buy my reas-surance?

"All I know," he said, "is that I have this job to finish and another I've just signed on. You're a flake—a talented flake—"

"I am not a flake!"

"A talented flake, but still a flake. And I have to keep my mind on business. I have a lot of ground to recover after the setbacks I suffered these last few years. I don't need the designer on this job, her nutty PI neighbor, and the nutty neighbor's cats to wind up in jail for harassing an innocent family in mourning."

"How about you audition for the *Looney Tunes* show?" I opened the door and stepped outside. He followed, so I added, "I haven't even seen Bella in days."

"But you will. Probably the minute she reads the paper."

"Nah. I bet she's too hot on the trail of lost dogs to even scope out the news."

"Don't forget. She's addicted to the news and gory cable cop shows. I bet she knows as much as you about Darlene and her family, if not more."

The lurching in my stomach? Well, it had taken a break, but now that he mentioned Bella, her hunger for news, and her unusual absence, it started to buck and roll with a vengeance.

"Gotta go," I said. "See ya."

I slid into my Honda, cranked it up, and pulled away from Tedd's office. I had a nutty neighbor to track down.

Among other things.

Like Cissy's financial situation. Anything and everything

about the Weikert brothers. The skeletons in Dr. Díaz's closet. And the perfect handwoven rug for Tedd's waiting room.

All that while I dodged Dutch's suspicion radar.

It wouldn't be easy. But then again, nothing good comes all that easy. At least not to me. But still . . .

A girl's gotta do what a girl's gotta do.

The only reaction I got when I rang Bella's doorbell was the maniacal meows of her two beasts. How a woman can wind up with two identical feral felines, each a potential clone of the other, is beyond me. I was a witness to Faux Bali's original appearance, but I still find it hard to believe the universe can encompass more than one Bali H'ai.

It's not as if Bella picked them out at the same cabbage patch on the same day, spawned from the same parental gene pool. No. She adopted the two at different times, several years apart, and, from what she says, in two different states of the nation.

What's worse, both monsters have it in for me. And while I'm fine with cats as a rule, I don't love these particular two. So I didn't hang around Bella's door for long.

She had to be off on a wild pet chase—I hoped. I was free to snoop . . . er . . . investigate.

And that's how I wound up at Weikert's Euro-Import Auto Sales. My Honda's only a couple of years old, and I don't want to replace it, no matter how many bucks Marge left me. But I am interested in foreign cars.

Mildly.

Minusculely.

Okay, okay. Hardly at all. But since I don't know a thing about them, I can honestly say there's much for me to learn. Which is what I told Tommy Weikert when he slithered out of his office.

His outfit looked just like the one of the other day, different only in color and fit—these pants bore pleats over his melon-shaped paunch.

"Hey! I know you," he bellowed with all the charm of a hungry cobra over the million-decibel Muzak. "You're the decorator. Too bad about my mom, huh? You didn't get the job after all."

Oh, Tommy charmed me, all right. He elicits the same fascination you experience during a horror movie, when you know something awful is about to happen, when you know you don't want to see it happen but you can't take your eyes away until it does.

Poor Darlene.

"I see you drive a Honda," he said with disdain. "I guess you've realized it's time to move up."

"Ah . . . I'm not sure."

"You will be after today."

Tommy shouldn't count chickens so soon. "We'll see."

He swept his shiny, maroon-satin-covered arm in a broad arc. "Anything in particular you like?"

"I'm afraid I don't know much about this kind of car . . ."

And he was off. I followed him, free to let my attention roam, to scope out the place, to take note of anything and everything my heart desired. The guy loves the sound of his voice.

But there wasn't much to notice. The showroom, while spiffy and spit-and-polish, was a Sahara but for the two of us. Tommy's inventory encompassed all of six vehicles: two Mercedes-Benzes, one a convertible, the other a traditional boxy sedan; one lime green Jaguar with a cigar-smoke-scented interior; a beige Beemer; a black Rolls; and some red Italian creation with a name without enough loop to catch on the hook part of my Velcro brain.

A tinny rendition of "Disco Duck" pinged out in a momentary lull of the relentless onslaught of Muzak. Tommy pulled out a cell phone and flashed me more teeth than I care to see.

"It's London." Big, fat, cheesy wink. "Gotta take this one, doll. Look around. Try the cars. See how they fit you."

London? Maybe London, Kentucky, or London, Texas. And the caller? Probably someone looking for his missing Jag. But I took the chance to check the odometer of each of the six cars. All had minimal mileage, but not a single vehicle was newer than four years. They couldn't all have been driven by a grandma to church on Sunday and nothing more.

Maybe my next stop would be at Larry's. I had no idea what the guy did or even where he lived. Time to let my fingers do the walking through the white pages.

"Tommy?"

He was too busy begging on the phone to answer me.

"Another month, man. Please. That's all I need. How

was I gonna know she was going to change everything at the last minute?"

Hmm . . . interesting tidbit.

Tommy's championship whining continued. "Hey, listen. I got a big buyer in the showroom right now. Some ritzy decorator. I bet she'll take the Bentley. You know, to drive rich clients around."

Yikes! Two big strikes against Tommy: one, there was no Bentley in the showroom, and two, if that was how he saw me, as the "big buyer," he was in worse shape than I'd thought. In more ways than one.

"Oh, all right," he grumped. "Two weeks, then. I'll sell the Bentley by then, and I can pay you back in two weeks."

That was my cue. "Tommy? Thanks for the info. You sure know your foreign cars. But I have to hurry home now. I'll give the car some more thought."

"No!" He ran to my side in panic. "See?" He slapped the clamshell phone shut. "I'm done. Now, which one's it gonna be? I'll bet I can guess. It's the Rolls. It's just so you."

Not in this lifetime. "I'll get back to you. But now I really have to hurry. So many walls, so much to faux. See ya!"

I ran. Yeah, I did the cowardly lion bit and split. I was afraid if I stayed there a minute longer, he'd tie me to the steering wheel of the Rolls and help himself to my debit card. This guy looked like hungry desperation and was a prime suspect in the mur—

Oh. Yeah. Darlene died of cancer.

That sorta deflated my sails, but it didn't slow my pace. My Honda was a welcome sight.

The gray fedora and tan trench up ahead? Not so
much.

I reached my car and thumped my head against the roof.
"Bella! What are you doing here?"

"How'd'ya know it was me?" she asked, indignant. "I'm
undercover."

"You showed me the cover, remember?"

"Oh yeah." Her brief disappointment vanished behind
a smile. "Toodle-ooh, then, Haley girl. I have a kill—ah . . .
er . . . killer headache, and I'd better head on home."

I nabbed the stubby tail of her trench's belt. "Not so fast,
Sherlock Cahill. You haven't answered my question. Why
are you here? Show me a cat or a dog in the middle of the
business district. A little old iguana or even a tarantula
will do."

She waved. "Oh, you'd be surprised. You have to scratch
the surface to find your culp—er . . . what you're looking
for, you know."

I tossed my backpack purse into my car and crossed my
arms. "What *are* you looking for?"

She matched my stance. "How about you?"

"I asked you first."

"I'll tell you after you tell me, Haley girl."

Mental scramble time. "I . . . ah . . . met Tommy Weikert
when I went to meet with his mother the day she died. I
was going to redesign her parlor."

"Yeah, I know. I read the paper. But what ya want with
him? Last time I checked, you said you loved your Honda

and didn't want some fancy doodadded hood for people to know you're loaded."

"I'm not buying one of those cars!"

"Then what are you doing here?"

Quick, quick. Think of something, Haley.

Only the funeral came to mind. "Um . . . the Weikert brothers asked Dad to do Darlene's funeral."

That's as far as I would go. But it seemed to work for Bella. At least for now.

"I see. You were on an errand."

Her easy acceptance left a funky taste in my mouth. "And now that I'm done, why don't I give you a ride home?"

"I have my car, and I have . . . my own errands to run. See ya!"

That belt tail came in handy again. "What happened to your headache?"

She slapped my hands away. "Oh, I took something for it earlier. It just kicked in."

"What about the Balis? How long have they been locked up?"

My question tinted her face with guilt. But then she squared her shoulders and smiled—a huge, all-the-way-around-her-head, everything's-just-too-cool-with-my-world kind of smile. "Oh, the babies are fine, Haley. You know I leave them lots of food, water, toys, and treats."

I didn't buy the smile. "Yes, you do leave them food, water, and treats, but it's you I'm sure they miss. You've been gone a long time."

She pulled herself to her full height. "I'm a working

mother now." Then she gave me a slit-eyed look. "Besides, how'd you know how long I've been gone? You been spying on me?"

"Of course not. I hadn't seen you in days, so I stopped by to make sure everything was all right. I'm not used to going this long without a Bella fix, you know."

"That's so sweet, Haley girl. I guess absence does make the heart grow longer, but I'm very busy these days. I have a couple of open cases, and I have to follow a mutedplicity of clues. So you're just going to have to live with it—like my babies."

Just what I was afraid of. "Care to tell me about your cases? I'm real interested."

That got me another serving of suspicious looks. "Nothing too complicated," Bella hedged. "You know, same old, same old in the life of a pet detective."

"My, my, my. Well, hello there, ladies. Fancy seeing you here, outside Weikert's Euro-Import Auto Sales. And together, no less. All that's missing is the Balis."

Sometimes I wish I was bigger, stronger, and of a pugilistic bent. Dutch Merrill lives because I'm none of the above.

I turned the tables on him. "And what are *you* doing here?"

"Aren't you the one who's always saying I have to do something about my beat-up old truck?"

I laughed. When I got control again, I said, "You're going to trade in the rolling wreck for a set of those overrated, overpriced, froufrou wheels. Hah! We don't live in lala land, so that doesn't even rise to the level of a lousy excuse. Give me a break, Merrill. Why are you really here?"

"Would you believe I didn't buy a word you said back at Tedd's?"

Groan. "I can't believe you said that. I don't lie."

His turn to laugh. "I'll give you that much. You don't lie, but you don't always tell it all."

"Hey, a girl's gotta keep a hint of mystery, you know." Good grief! Where had *that* come from?

Bella clapped. "Woo-hoo! You go, Haley girl. Keep him hooked and guessing. You'll reel him in in no time."

I'd forgotten I had my shadow at my side, so I ducked into my Honda. "I don't want to reel anyone in. Especially not him."

"You could do worse," Dutch ventured.

I slammed the door shut. "I don't have time for this."

He leaned his forearms on the roof of the car. "You really don't, Haley. Quit nosing around where there's nothing to sniff."

"Ah . . ." Bella began to bustle down the street. "See ya, kids. It's been real!"

I banged my forehead against the steering wheel—Bella and Dutch inspire lots of head banging. "She is snooping."

"I told you." When I glared, he held up a warning finger. "But you are too. So cut it out. There's nothing to snoop about. You can see how crazy Bella looks on one of her lurk missions."

"I don't wear vintage hats and tan coats."

"That's not what I mean, and you know it."

"I don't have to put up with this. I'm going home. Where I have a mountain of sewing to do for our joint project."

He rapped his knuckles against the car door, then stepped away. "Remember. Nothing happened this time. The woman was sick. You have an obligation to Tedd. You promised her you'd do her proud. Don't let her down."

As he walked away, I remembered making that promise. But not just to Tedd.

I'd promised Darlene Weikert I wouldn't let her down. True, I'd spoken about the redesign of her home. But things had changed. Darlene had affected me. I felt a certain responsibility toward her.

Didn't that mean I had to put my suspicions to rest? Everyone said she'd died of natural causes.

Or would I let her down if I just gave up?

Lord? What should I do?

5

I'd just been compared to Bella—for the second time. First Dad, now Dutch. Something about it threw me—it was very uncool. Not that Bella's not a totally cool older woman, because she is. But there is that nuttiness.

And I'm no flake. Contrary to Dutch's opinion.

These thoughts zoomed through my mind on my way home. I considered a stop at the *dojo* but thought better of it at the last minute. I can't keep a single solitary secret from Tyler Colby, *sensei* extraordinaire and friend for life. I wasn't ready to share my concerns yet.

The more I learned about Darlene Weikert, her friends, and her family, the stronger the possibility of murder seemed. Yes, cancer can be a swift, ruthless killer, but Darlene hadn't looked that sick when we met. And I should know; I watched my mother waste away from liver cancer that developed secondary to hepatitis.

I also couldn't forget Cissy's comment about Darlene's recent weight gain. A woman about to succumb to cancer wouldn't gain weight; she might bloat from medication, but Darlene hadn't looked bloated. She'd had what looked like normal color in her face, and I remembered her eyes as clear too.

It was too much for me to figure out.

Well, Lord. No one else seems to give much thought to Darlene's sudden death other than Bella and me. And while I know that matchup doesn't much favor me, I did have my doubts from the start. Bella just jumped in after she read that story in the paper. She can't stand to be anywhere but moving and shaking in the middle of the action.

At the manse, I pulled into the driveway and parked. *Indecision* and *waffling* aren't words that describe my normal tendencies, but that's where I was right about then.

So, Father. Here's the deal. Do I do like everyone says and just forget the whole thing? Or do I follow my instincts and check things out a little more?

As usual, I didn't hear a Charlton Heston voice from above. Too bad God doesn't work that way, doesn't yell at you what you should do. Life down here would be way easier if he did.

I think.

So I'm on my own. Well, I do have your Word, and I guess that's my next stop.

A sense of peace filled me at the thought of the comfort I always find in Scripture. God might not boom out directions, but his Word never, ever fails.

I headed straight for my room, took my Bible, and sat in my chaise lounge, right by the window. I spent a good, long time there, soaked in verse after verse, then dropped to my knees for some heavy-duty praise and prayer.

When I stood again, I glanced out the window and saw Bella drive her eighteen-wheeler-sized vintage pink Caddie into her driveway. She bustled up the walk, unlocked the door, and scooted inside, where I'm sure her maniacal mousers welcomed her with what passes as affection from those two.

Downstairs, I went through the motions of dinner prep, my mind on the Weikerts the whole time. While Tommy was a major sleaze, all I knew about Larry was that he didn't think much of his brother and dressed in rejects from a recycle center's ragbag.

When Dad came in, I served the meal, ate robotlike, and communicated with "Uh-huhs" and "Reallys?" The more time passed, the more I knew I had to check out Larry Weikert.

If only I knew where to find the geek . . . er . . . guy.

Since there couldn't be too many Weikerts in the phone book, I started there. No luck. But then I had a brainstorm. The guy looked like the poster boy for computer nerddom. It brought to mind the Internet. There are those cyber white pages sites that give out addresses with no sense of guilt at the intrusion they've made into people's privacy.

The minute I typed in the guy's name, Google had a field day. And the white pages were the least of it. Sure enough, Larry boy was the fair-haired child of the blogger world, king of the cyberwonks. He evidently did nothing that couldn't be done via computer.

I had his snail mail address in seconds.

Although I'm not often given to rationalization, I figured that if God didn't want me to check out Larry Weikert, he wouldn't have made my search so easy. My decision was made.

"Ah . . . Dad?" I snagged my backpack purse on my way to the front door. "I have to run out for a little while. I need to do some . . . um . . . research, so don't worry if I'm not back right away. Love ya, and bye!"

Before Dad could object or pepper me with questions, I ran out, plopped into my car, and sped down the street. Larry lived on Seagull Court, one of the older streets in tiny Wilmont, one where homes had hit lean times a while back. Most of the large, family-size structures had long been converted into apartments, and a slew of college kids rented them for peanuts.

I'd never peddle my services around here.

When I pulled up to 1569 Seagull Court, I was surprised to find a tiny shotgun-style house with a second story plopped on the first like a brooding hen on a nest of eggs. Its two stories probably didn't add up to more than 850 to 900 square feet of living space. But it stood alone, and that said a lot: Larry's place, the Taj Mahal of Seagull Court. Interesting.

I parked at the end of the street and settled in to wait. What for? I didn't know. I figured sooner or later something would come to me.

And it did. In the person of the delivery guy.

"Oh yeah! It's a party, it's a party."

Okay. So I quote corny stuff, but hey! It can come in handy.

Maybe I could get in to look around if I posed as a delivery girl. At the very least, if someone caught me snooping outside, I'd have a . . . maybe excuse.

I accosted the kid right before he stepped onto the front stoop of Larry's place. I sniffed. Soy sauce and garlic and all other good things—yum!

"Here," I said with an overzealous smile. "I'll take that—"

I caught a glimpse of the box. "Nike?"

He shrugged. "We're out of bags tonight. Besides, shoe boxes work better. They don't rip so much."

"Okay. Anyway, I'll take it. I'm so hungry I could eat a bear, but Chinese'll taste better, I'm sure. How much do I owe you?"

"You're not the guy who called the order in. What's up with that?"

Lucky for me, it was dark and he couldn't see me blush. "Nothing. Nothing at all. I just want to surprise him is all. You know. We haven't seen each other for days, and I figure this'll be . . . I don't know. Fun?"

At first he looked even more doubtful. Then he must have had a lightbulb moment. "Oh, I get it. It's one of those chick things. Guys don't get it, but you do it anyway. You women are crazy. All right. It's sixteen twenty-five."

"Larry must've been hungry," I said before I could stop myself. I gave the boy a twenty and a nervous laugh.

He shook his head and left. I heard him mutter, "Crazy chick." I had to agree.

What to do with a Nike shoe box of really hot cartons until I scope out the territory?

What? What next, Haley?

I looked around, stunned by the smorgasbord of louder-than-loud music that exploded out of windows next door—on both sides—across the street, to the rear, and even from the ratty Yugo that spit and sputtered down the street. I heard reggae, rap, and rock. Beneath that, New Age and jazz gave the cacophony of words a base coat of melody. And if I tried really, really hard, I could pick out a thin gloss of Mozart, which added to the bizarre feel of the place.

As much as I wished the music were the score to a movie of my life story, complete with script and director to tell me what to do next, I was as clueless as before.

Hot grease seeped through the shoe box onto my hand.

What to do? What to do?

Well, I sure wasn't about to learn anything helpful as a human kung pao stand, so I decided to check out the house. Why? I don't know. It just seemed *the* thing in movies and TV shows, and since I didn't have a script of my own, I figured I'd take a page from theirs. Besides, I think better when I'm doing something.

I went to the pencil-thin aisle of grass on the right-hand side of the house. It ran straight to the rear, where a monster tree blocked the way. That's when I finally got a clue.

Up on the second floor and toward the back, yellowy

light speared out from a window and into the night sky. A hefty branch of that lovely, lovely tree spread out oh so very, very close by.

Serendipity!

Maybe I wouldn't have to come face-to-face with Larry after all, moo shoo whatever in hand.

I dropped the fragrant shoe box at the foot of the tree and called on my tree-climbing skills, skills I hadn't used for years—at least fourteen. To my relief, they came back fast, especially since I was motivated.

Hidden by the lush thicket of leaves, I scooched my behind onto the branch and inched forward as far as I dared. Then I parted some of the greenery.

"Oh, wow . . ."

I was stunned, amazed, stupefied. I'd never seen anything like it. Good grief! I couldn't have imagined it, no matter how wild my imagination.

Larry Weikert had more electronics stuffed in one small room than I'd seen in my entire life. NASA had nothing on the man. He had stuff hooked up with enough wires to light up New York, Chicago, LA, Dallas, and Seattle—all at one time. I stared in horrified fascination.

Hands on one of the multitude of keyboards, Larry typed at a feverish rate. He then spun to face another wall covered in monitors and stacks of black boxes adorned with wires, buttons, and disk-eating maws. He flicked a slender silver lever, checked a screen above his head, then reached for the keyboard and beat out another bunch of stuff.

Icons scrambled across the screen he'd checked, then

morphed into a pair of lists. Curious, I widened my peep-hole, leaned forward, and saw it wasn't words but numbers in one of the columns. Unless I was way wrong, it looked like Larry had pulled up the activity in a bank account or maybe a business's financial transactions.

He seemed fixated on this particular screen. He stood, ran a hand through his thinning hair, then pushed his glasses up to his forehead and rubbed his eyes. Something didn't seem to add up for him. What? I didn't know.

But I was determined to find out.

Mindful of my precarious perch but also aware of the solid thickness of the tree limb, I decided to scooch a couple of inches closer to the window.

"Mmmrrrreooooow!"

At the sound of that familiar feral cry, I jerked. I dropped through empty space, scrambled for a handhold on leaves, twigs, anything my sheltering tree might offer. I found nothing.

Splat!

"Yuck!" At least I didn't land on my butt.

My Birkenstock offered no protection against the sticky, slithery ooze of saucy Chinese once my foot tore through the flimsy protection of the steam-dampened cardboard lid. So much for the delivery kid's faith in Nike shoe boxes. Hope the spiffy shoes hold up better.

Above me, still on my branch, Bali H'ai—or maybe Faux Bali, who can tell?—kept up her off-key contribution to the musical stew of Seagull Court. I'm sure it was nothing less than hysterical laughter on her part. She got me, all right.

I hobbled in a hurry toward my Honda, determined to rid myself of my very first piece of Nike footwear. Hobble, hobble, hobble, stick out my leg, and shake, shake, shake. Mushrooms and pea pods and rice littered the walkway in my wake.

Lovely.

Elegant.

Sophisticated—just the look every up-and-coming interior designer wants as she goes down the street.

Yeah right.

But I couldn't take the time to stop, yank off the box lid, and scrape away the remains of Larry's dinner. I had to make my escape, and fast. Because wherever Bali is, Bella can't be far behind. I didn't want her to see me shackled by soy-sauced noodles and soggy cardboard. Especially not after I'd warned her against snooping.

By now I was sure not just Larry but also the whole free world had heard Bali, my disgraceful descent from the tree, and my subsequent landing in the food.

So much for stealthy snooping.

I really, really had to split. Right then. No matter how much sauce and starch I smeared onto my gas pedal. I hobbled faster.

And ran headfirst into an aftershave-scented wall. Big hands manacled my shoulders. "Not so fast," a well-known voice said. "I thought you were too busy to go off like Bella on one of her 'missions.'"

"Ah . . . er . . . I was . . . oh yeah. Right. I had to deliver something—"

"Give it up, Haley. I followed you from your house. I saw you accost the delivery kid, watched you pay for the egg foo yong. Sure, at that point, you had Larry's dinner to deliver, so you didn't technically lie. Then you climbed the tree. You know? You're almost as fast as Bali, going up and coming down to obliterate the chop suey."

I sputtered.

He covered my mouth. Then he added insult to injury. "I had to watch you turn into Wilmont's latest Peeping Tom. Can you imagine how the headline would've gone over if the cops had caught you looking in Larry Weikert's window?"

Oops! "It never crossed my mind—"

"Did anything cross your mind? Besides your loony idea that this man had something to do with his mother's death, that is."

He had me there. I was thankful for the cover of darkness so he couldn't see my dismay. That's when a zillion floodlights beamed on. In the dark I'd missed the evidence of Larry's paranoia; the roof of the house was wired to the hilt. What is his deal?

I winced at the assault on my eyes. "Oh, okay. You busted me, all right? So. What're you going to do about it, Merrill?"

"I'm going to watch you get in your car; then I'm going to follow you home. And just so you don't get any more crazy ideas, I'm going to be on you closer than your shadow. You need a keeper."

Super. "Oh, that won't be necessary—"

"You don't have to do that!" Wilmont's pet detective cut in. "I'm on the job already."

Dutch and I groaned.

"Bella," I muttered.

"Bella," he echoed.

A door with squeaky hinges opened. "What's coming down out there?"

The three of us spun toward the front of the house. Larry, in another message T-shirt and ratty jeans, glared from the doorway, his nondescript features twisted in anger. "What are you people doing on my property? Can't you read? I have 'No Trespassing' signs everywhere."

I looked where he pointed and saw his signs, the ones I hadn't noticed before. "Ah . . . Larry? Do you remember me? I'm the interior designer who had an appointment with your mother the day she died—"

"What? Are you nuts?" Dutch's question came out as a low growl. "That was dumb. Why identify yourself? Now he can sic the cops on you."

"Hey, Lila and her Smurfs don't scare me anymore. They did their worst, and I lived through it." I turned back to my quarry turned irate home owner. "Um . . . you asked my father to do your mother's funeral, but he told me you and your brother owed him a hymn and some Scriptures so he can write his sermon. At dinner he said you hadn't done it yet."

"I know nothing about hymns and verses. He must've talked to my brother. Tommy doesn't live here. Hey! Is that my moo goo gai pan you're standing on?"

Yet another of the innumerable awkward moments in the life of Haley Farrell. I gave the mess another shake, but the box lid didn't budge. "I . . . had a small accident."

"What kind of accident do you have with Chinese that hasn't been delivered? And how do you wind up with it on your foot?"

"It's perfectly logicable," Bella said. "Haley fell out of your tree."

Larry's eyes looked ready to pop from their sockets. "What were you doing in my tree?"

"I . . . ah—"

"Mmmrrrrreooooow!"

"There!" I exclaimed, relieved to finally find a use for Bali H'ai. "See the cat? She belongs to my elderly neighbor here. I . . . was on that branch—with her, you understand—and slipped. That's how I landed on the food."

"I'm disappointed," my albatross whispered. "I've heard you do so much better."

"What's up with that, Haley girl? You didn't go get Bali," Bella said, indignant. "Bali went up to fetch you."

"What was my dinner doing by the tree?"

"Okay," I said. "I'm outta here. You guys can sort it all out together. This is too weird even for me."

"Wait!" Bella cried, in a hurry to catch up to me. "You can't leave. What about the murder?"

Larry gasped. "What?"

Dutch groaned. "Not again."

"She died of cancer, Bella," I said in an attempt at normalcy. "You can go home too."

"Murder?" Larry asked, his eyes narrowed. He trotted over. "Cancer? Is she talking about my mother?"

I gave up. The curb looked like a great place to sit and remove the cardboard shackle. Off my foot, the scraps looked even more pathetic. "Sorry—"

Larry's look cut off my apology.

"Terrific," he muttered when he glanced farther down. "That's my lo mein you smushed too. So much for dinner." He pointed at Bella. "About her. Does she think my mother was murdered?"

I sighed. "I'm afraid she does."

Dutch snickered and came over to join the circus. "So does our dinner killer."

"I do not—"

"Watch it!" he said. "You're going to blow your no lies streak."

"Don't you have somewhere else you have to be?" I blew a disobedient curl off my forehead. "And yes, Larry. Bella does think your mother was murdered, but that's because she just got her private investigator license and thinks there's a crime under every toadstool, boulder, and leaf."

"I do not," Bella argued, fists on hips. "And you're the one who started the investigating. I'm just following up— you know, double-checking the clues to make sure you don't wind up in trouble like the last two times."

Larry looked ill. "Two times? You do this on a regular basis? How many other Chinese dinners have you trashed?"

I stood. "It's my first and last. I'm going home."

This time no one tried to stop me. I walked away with

what few shreds of dignity I could call up. But when I reached the Honda, Larry spoke up again.

"Tell you what. If you women think my mother was murdered, you need to check out Cissy. She's the one who shot Mom up with all that bogus stuff from Mexico, and she stole more than half of it for herself."

My jaw nearly clipped the sidewalk.

"Cissy?" I asked when I forced my mouth to work again.

"Yeah, lady. Cissy. She's nuttier than peanut butter. She hooked Mom up with that Mexican quack, and I'm not sure she did it to help Mom either. I think she just wanted a free ride to the stuff for herself. And hey. If she could get the terminal patient to change the will in her favor while she was at it, then that's just the cherry on the Cissy fruitcake sundae's top, you know?"

I knew Cissy had injected Darlene with the HGH, but she hadn't mentioned her use of the stuff. "Does Cissy have cancer too?"

Larry laughed. "Not unless common sense can grow malignancies."

"Why would she want to take the stuff, then?"

Anger returned to Larry's face. "Because she's nuts. Because she's bought all the wacky science out there about that hormone stuff. Because she thinks if she takes HGH, she'll live forever, and if there's one thing Cissy Grover's scared of, it's death."

He really didn't like Cissy, did he? Did he have a point? Had he checked her out electronically? What had those two columns told him? What had he seen on that computer screen? Did it reflect on Cissy? Or on him?

If it put him in a bad light, did it incriminate him enough that he'd cast suspicion on a retired nurse with an unconventional passion and an unhealthy fear of death?

The technology in that room cost beaucoup bucks. Who knew how many computers he had in that setup. Or even elsewhere in the house. Where did Larry get the money to pay for all his hardware?

Cissy had said the brothers had gone through their trust funds in record time back when Darlene turned over the accounts to them. Did Larry go way berserk with his techie purchases then? More recently? Did he owe the wrong kind of guy for the toys in the überwired playroom?

I still had a crucial question for him. "Do *you* think your mother was murdered?"

With a strangled sound deep in his throat, Larry turned and jogged back to his house. Without another word, he slammed the door shut. Seconds later all the lights went out.

That was my cue. I didn't say good-bye to my tails.

I left, suspicion growing moment by moment into certainty. I didn't need a coroner's report. I didn't need the police's official cause of death. Now I knew something, something concrete, even though I didn't know how I knew it.

Darlene Weikert hadn't died from her disease. Someone had helped her along on her final trip. And no one believed it. No one but Larry, Bella, and me.

It was time to talk to Lila.

Even if it killed me.

6

"You need help," Lila said the next morning.

"Yours."

"I don't think so. The department pays me to investigate homicides, not delusions."

I slapped her desktop. "I'm not delusional, Lila. Don't you get it? It's too easy, too tied up. Nothing in life comes out that squeaky clean. What better cover could a killer ask for than his victim's terminal cancer?"

Lila rounded her desk and came to my side. "I'll grant you that would be the perfect way to . . . well, get away with murder. But that's not what happened here. Dr. Hamilton, the victim's oncologist at the Fred Hutchinson Cancer Institute, concurs with the coroner. Darlene Weikert was in the final stages of the disease. She lost her battle with cancer."

I stood toe-to-toe with the deceptively delicate detective. "I might have bought that if I hadn't met her sons, if I hadn't learned about her Mexican contraband hormone, if I didn't know about the massive loan she made to the south-of-the-border doc, if I didn't know about Cissy Grover's fascination with HGH and fear of death. Get the picture?"

The tiny flare of the detective's nostrils told me I'd surprised her.

"You've been busy—again." Lila crossed her arms. "But are you suggesting my officers and I are so inept we don't know these details? Because I can assure you, we aren't, and we do."

"And you don't think there's something fishy about Darlene's death? Even with all those facts staring you in the face?"

"Haley, the woman had cancer."

"I didn't say she didn't. I know she had cancer. I accept it. It's all those other things that make me wonder if she really did die from the cancer. She could've been killed—by someone, not the disease. Tell me. Did I hear you say the coroner did an autopsy?"

"The executrix of Mrs. Weikert's estate requested one."

"Oh." I hadn't expected that from Cissy—a suspect. "Okay. And the results . . . ?"

"Nothing unusual, aside from the haemangiosarcoma of the liver."

"Is there a way to check to see if someone suffocated her?"

Lila tapped the toe of her oh-so-chic left shoe. "The autopsy did look for asphyxiation but found no evidence of petechial bleeding."

"Pe . . . who?"

"Petechia are tiny red or purple spots on the eyes, face,

lungs, and neck that appear when asphyxiation causes small areas of subcutaneous bleeding. Their presence suggests suffocation but not necessarily strangulation."

The technobabble made my head spin. "Okay. If you say so."

"*I* don't say so. The coroner says so."

So much for that idea. "How about poisoning?"

"There was no reason to test for poisoning. The corpse showed no evidence of possible poisoning."

I winced. "Do you have to call her 'the corpse'?"

Lila sighed. "Haley, in my line of work I come across a number of Mrs. Weikerts. If I didn't separate myself from them, I'd have been locked up in a psych ward long ago. I have to focus on the crime, not the nice or nasty person who became a victim."

"I understand. But what I don't get is why no one ran a tox screen for poison. Could you . . . enlighten me again?"

Lila's patronizing expression didn't sit well with me. Not that the smart remark I'd almost made would've sat well with her either. But I'm not all that stupid. I didn't argue; I wanted that answer.

"In most cases of death by poison," she said, "we find evidence at the time of death. Either the body shows characteristics of the poison's presence or the crime scene reveals evidence of a questionable substance. We then test to find a match."

"So you don't test in a plain-vanilla suspicious death? One where the person dies out of the blue for no apparent reason?"

"I did look around the room, and Mrs. Weikert *didn't* die out of the blue or for no apparent reason. The woman died of liver cancer."

We'd waltzed down this path before, but the band still played the same tune. "Yes, Lila, Darlene had liver cancer. But is there some way to know for sure if the cancer itself killed her? All by itself. With no help from anyone or anything else."

"Do you mean a lab test that would determine whether the actual malignancy was without any doubt the immediate cause of death as opposed to something else?"

"Something like that."

Lila shook her head, a faint frown on her brow. "I'd never given that much thought. But I've never heard of a test that can prove or disprove whether a particular disease the victim suffered was the actual cause of death to the complete exclusion of other potential causes. The medical community presupposes the terminal disease as the cause of death. In the absence of evidence otherwise, that is."

"Hmm . . . you mean that the medical and law enforcement communities just assume that a victim dies because the victim suffers from a terminal disease?"

She pressed her lips thin. Then, "That's what I said."

"It sounds like the cop shop version of ring-around-the-rosy, and it's stupid."

"I beg your pardon?"

"Sure, I know the terminal disease is the cause of just about every one of those deaths, but I'd bet at least one in every thousand or so is a murder. A murder you guys didn't bother to check out because the victim had a terminal disease. Tell me that's not dumb."

"I've never thought of it that way," Lila said, another frown on her brow. "Theoretically, I suppose you could be right, but practically? I don't think so."

"Why? Because I'm an interior designer and not a cop or a doc?"

"No." The detective glanced at her watch. "Because years—centuries—of experience provide us with a wealth of evidence that points to either natural death or murder when specific sets of indicators are present."

That brief check of the time and her oh-so-stuffy talk told me I'd overstayed my questionable welcome. "Okay, Lila. I yield to your superior knowledge. And since neither you nor I have a truckload of time to waste, I'll head on out. But do me a favor, please?"

With a Mount Rainier's worth of reluctance, Lila nodded.

"Please, *please*, consider the possibility of murder by poison in Darlene's case. Too many people stand to make out like bandits from her wealth now that she's gone. Or at any rate, too many people thought they stood to gain from her death."

"Trust me, Haley. Go ahead, give it a try. The rest of Wilmont does. Keep in mind, we checked out all Mrs. Weikert's friends and family. There's nothing there. You can go home and get back to . . ." she gestured in a vague, distracted way ". . . get back to whatever you designer types do."

I gave her the benefit of my expert eye rolling. "Now

there's a patronizing statement. I thought better of you, Detective Tsu."

"You're right." The detective sat back at her desk. "I apologize for the comment. But you really should focus on your business and let me focus on mine."

Ouch! "You told me, all right. See ya."

I left the cop shop no more convinced than when I first arrived. You always hear on TV, especially on the news, that when someone dies under suspicious circumstances, it's a no-brainer to follow the money. But if you were to try to follow Darlene's money, you'd have to run around everyone in her immediate circle.

Which meant I had a lot of circling to do.

No matter what Lila or Dutch said.

I knew what my gut said.

It hollered, "Murder."

I'd let a ton of bookkeeping pile up at the Norwalk & Farrell Auctions warehouse. But before I went there, I wanted to change into hands-on designer garb. I planned to stop by Tedd's office later on. I had to make sure the stain I'd chosen did what I hoped it would on the actual boards Mr. Watanabe had delivered.

At home, I wrote a note to tell Dad he either had to scavenge in the fridge for dinner or maybe hit a Golden Arches type of emporium. I had enough catch-up work to keep my nose to the grindstone for a month of nights or more.

But I was ambushed before I got away.

"Okay, Haley girl. Now you have to listen to me."

"I do?"

Her smug smile gave me the willies. She was up to something—trouble, since it was Bella.

"You do. I have proof."

Oh boy. "Proof? What kind of proof? And of what?"

"Proof that Darlene Weikert was murdered."

I closed my eyes, counted to twenty—I didn't have time for a million. "Go home, Bella. I just left Lila Tsu. We discussed every last little detail of Darlene's death. There's nothing there."

I didn't have to let her into my gut's secret scream, did I?

Bella *hmphed.* "That shows how much you and the detective know. I took the time to meet Cissy Grover. I really like her, but that's my problem."

"Problem? What kind of problem can you possibly have with Cissy?"

"Well, I like her. But she killed Darlene."

"What?"

Bella's jet black Brillo Pad hair did a disco dance with each nod. "Cissy killed Darlene. I figured it all out thanks to my mail-order college courses. She killed Darlene 'cause she got Darlene to change her will. She wanted the money. And you know what? She was snitching Darlene's drugs. You know, that MGM—"

"HGH, Bella. It stands for human growth hormone."

"Whatever. Anyway, Darlene didn't know Cissy was using her stuff. She had a nifty little racket going. Darlene considered Cissy her best friend, but Cissy was more like a tick, sucking out Darlene's dope and dough."

"Ah . . . there's a little problem with your theory, Bella. What happens to Cissy's supply of HGH now that Darlene's gone? Don't you think she'd rather have her steady supplier alive? The money's still tied up in probate, since the sons are going to contest the will."

"No big deal. You see, Darlene gave Cissy tons of money in the last six months, something like ten grand. That buys plenty of that kind of dope."

"And how'd you find that out?"

"She told me."

"You got Cissy to talk about her personal business with a perfect stranger?"

"Oh, we're not perfect strangers. Not anymore. We're friends now. And that's my problem. How'm I going to turn her into Wilmont's next pet detective if they lock her up? I'm good but not that good."

"Cissy Grover's going into the pet detective business?"

"Well, she needs to earn a living until her money goes through prostate, doesn't she?"

Sometimes it's best to ignore Bella's bloopers. "And you think it's a good idea to hire a woman you're sure killed her best friend."

Bella shrugged. "What can I say? I feel bad for her. She's really broken up about Darlene's death. Plus, that Jacob's a real handful, with that Alzheimer's getting worse every day. And Darlene's bratty sons are more trouble than a splinter in the butt."

No way was I going to touch that Bellaism. Not even with a ten-foot pole. "Bella! Think about it. You're sure

Cissy is a killer. And you go and offer her a job? What are you, nuts?"

Bella planted her fists on her Lifesaver-roll hips. "Watch it there, missy. You tell me a better way to keep an eye on a suspect."

"Gee, I don't know. Let's keep an eye on a suspect—oh, and let's give her the chance to work her way to murder number two: yours!"

"She won't hurt me. Remember. I'm" —she struck a really bad pose— "a martian artist."

"Yeah, you're an alien life force, all right." Bella had yet to earn her yellow belt, the first level up for beginners. "I've got to let Lila in on your latest. Maybe she can send a couple of her giant Smurfs to look out for you."

"Suit yourself. Just remember to tell her about Cissy. You know, that she killed Darlene."

I could just hear Lila. "I won't forget. I do have to give her a reason for your need for protection."

Other than rampant lunacy, that is. Bella needs protection from herself, and I often do the job, but this time she'd gone beyond even my powers. "Just don't do anything stupid."

Or nothing even more stupid than making someone you're sure already killed once your bestest new buddy.

"I'll be fine, Haley girl. You'll see. Perry Mason? Columbo? Sherlock Holmes? Pshaw!" She winked. "They can't keep up with me. Me and Jessica Fletcher."

Dear Lord, I've heard people say you watch out for children and fools, so could you please put in a little overtime on Bella here?

I let her go. What else could I do? Besides trust God to protect her.

Well, I also had to turn to Lila. And that was no piece of cake. Imagine our conversation. It was almost as insane as Bella's and mine.

"Come on, Lila," I said after we went around and around for about ten minutes on the phone. "Just think about it. Did Darlene really give Cissy all that money? Or did Cissy help herself to a mammoth piggy bank? She did steal the serum. And if she stole the money like she stole the serum, don't you think she might have gone all the way and killed Darlene? It's not that far a stretch."

In the end Lila assured me one of her officers had checked out Cissy's finances, and while she was broke, she'd recently paid off a hefty chunk of debt, something around the ten-thousand-dollar mark. Plus, she'd confessed the theft of the serum and admitted asking Darlene for the loan, which she said Darlene refused to call anything but a gift. Aside from her job with the Weikerts and a tiny trickle of Social Security, Cissy had no other visible means of support.

She hadn't lied to Bella about that.

But—and it was a big but—had she told all there was to tell about her finances? Was she hiding more debt? Maybe a gambling problem or something like that? Was that what Larry had checked out last night? How was I going to know?

Even if I someday got the chance to sneak into his cyberlab, I wouldn't know how to turn on one of those monster computers much less decipher the gobbledygook they

might reveal. And I had no access to private banking information—to my regret. But a hacker did, and the minor
matter of ethics wouldn't bother him. That's why Larry's
behavior made my suspicious mind hum.

Lord? How'm I going to figure this one out?

But there was nothing for me to figure out right then. I
had work to do. So I hit the road and went on to the warehouse, where an avalanche of paperwork threatened to
bury me alive.

I got nowhere with the paperwork. My mind behaved
like a carefree flea. It bounced from one juicy topic to another, none of which had a thing to do with my work. After
an hour and a half of that, I gave up. Maybe it was time to
turn over the paperwork to Ozzie. My partner is more than
capable. But the idea did dump a truckload of guilt on me.
I felt I was failing Marge, the woman who'd left everything
she owned in my care.

So I did nothing. Nothing other than lock up my flyspeck
of an office and head for Tedd's. Maybe the floor and stain
would hold my attention.

And maybe Tedd had some useful info I could shake
loose. Darlene had been her client. They might have talked
about Cissy, money, the doctor, the sons. It couldn't hurt
to ask.

It didn't hurt, but it didn't help either.

"I can't answer your questions, Haley. You know that.
She was my client."

"*Was* being the operative word here, Tedd. The woman's dead."

Tedd walked down the hall—yep, the one with the carved-door art. "I don't feel I can breach the confidentiality of a woman who can't give me permission."

"That's really lame, Tedd. I doubt even the law would hold you to that."

"Doubt away, my friend." She picked up a length of maple floorboard. "Please tell me my floor's not going to wind up looking this pale. With all the traffic it gets, it would look like dirt in a day or two."

I knew a diversionary tactic when I was on the receiving end of one. "That's where the stain comes in. It'll darken the maple to just the right shade. You won't recognize it when I'm done."

She handed me the board. "Go to it, then, designer woman. I want to see you do your magic on my floor."

And I wanted info she didn't want to give. So I packed up my disappointment and went to work. An hour later I'd tweaked enough to be happy with the results. I'd tried a couple different individual stains, then wound up mixing two of them to nail the color I really wanted. I knew I'd done the deed when Tedd walked out of her inner sanctum and pointed to my latest test piece.

"That's perfect!"

"I agree. I was about to take it in to you. This is dark enough to hide some dirt but light enough that the ebonized Guatemalan chairs will pop."

"Maybe it's time for you to pop on home too. I'm sure your father's wondering what happened to you."

"I left him a note. He knew I was coming over here to work for a while."

"That's good. But I'm on my way home, and I don't like to leave you here alone."

Tedd and I went through the same particularly ugly experience in our pasts. We were both victims of violent crime. Neither one of us takes safety for granted. "Not a problem, Doc. I'm tired and have a long day ahead of me tomorrow."

"I know what you mean. Mine's going to be rough too. But I won't be here. I've scheduled a day trip out of town. A short flight, business to deal with, and another hop back. No matter how short those flights are, though, they always tire me out."

"Hope it goes well for you."

"And I hope you sleep well."

It's a real pain to have your therapist for a friend. She knows you too well. "Yes, Dr. Rodriguez. I'll do my best to sleep."

And I did. I slept, rare though that is for me. But my dreams were filled with visions of Bella and her Balis kickboxing with little green men.

7

Saturday morning it rained. Sure, it rains all the time in the Pacific Northwest. But it's usually a misty deal or a shower in the middle of the day. Then it dries up. This Saturday, though, it rained. A steady flow of water poured down from the steel sky, and the air took an unpleasant nip out of you with every passing breeze.

Plus, it was Saturday. Saturdays mean something different to me than to the general population. To me, Saturdays mean missionary society meetings. Now, while I love all the missionary society does, and I am its biggest supporter with prayer, encouragement, direction, and funding, I do hate the meetings. I especially hate the need to run them. I'm not the best president the society has ever had, not by a long shot. The best would be my late mother.

After Mom died, a group of the members decided—don't ask me why—that I was the only possible candidate to succeed her. After a lot of velvet bullying, and even more objecting on my part, the ladies made the inevitable a reality. They voted me in, unanimously but for one.

Penelope Harham, Wilmont's postal clerk, has always coveted the position—go figure. It's all about paperwork, agendas, future projects, and those meetings. I'm supposed to make sure they run as planned, but it tends to become something like herding cats. And trust me. Its power doesn't rival that of the White House.

But in Penny's universe—scary place!—that presidency is *it*, and she's the only one who should occupy the spot. She never lets me forget how lousy I am at it either.

But it was still my responsibility. So I dragged myself out of bed, even when my every cell demanded I do the mole thing in my blankets. I pushed myself through a too-short if thorough shower, dressed, slipped my golden retriever an appeasing—I hoped—doggy cookie, and then dashed across the church's parking lot.

I screeched in just as the donated grandfather clock sang out nine bass *bongs*.

"You made it in time!" Ina Appleton, the society's welcome committee's chair, handed me a mug of Starbucks House Blend. She always brews some for me. "And guess who's late?"

"No way!" I looked around the room. "Are you serious?"

"I wouldn't kid about it. Penny's not here yet. It's a first."

"Wow. I never thought I'd see the day."

"You never thought you'd see what day?" the snippy woman in question asked.

Ina and I swapped glances.

She stepped back.

I stretched for an answer. "Ah . . . when rain really got on my nerves."

Penny narrowed her black eyes. "Are you sure you weren't indulging in sinful gossip?"

I opened my eyes to their fullest. "Who? *Moi?* Gotta tell you, Sister Penny, I'm not feeling the love here."

Ina scurried to the refreshment table while Penny seemed at a loss for a snotty retort. I didn't give her a chance to find one.

"If you don't mind, the members expect me at the podium. You got here a few minutes late, and I'd rather the delay not grow any longer."

I left her gaping. And while I don't normally treat people to that kind of mouthy disrespect, and I did feel a twinge of guilt at my atypical behavior, maybe Penny now knows how it feels to be at the wrong end of her snipes.

The podium is not one of my favorite things. I'd much rather arrange the chairs in a circle to put everyone more at ease. But since the podium/lectern/gavel route is how the society has done things since before Noah and his flood, I had no choice but to park myself up there.

The added height did do one thing: it gave me a bird's-eye view of the room. As a result, I couldn't miss the latest arrival . . . arrivals. I nearly swallowed my tongue.

"Bell—" I rivaled a screech owl. I cleared my throat and tried again. "Bella?"

My devious neighbor gave me a carefree little wave. "Hey there, Haley girl."

"Would you please come up here a minute?"

The Brillo Pad hair shook side to side.

I nodded.

The rest of the missionary society craned their necks and stared.

"Oh, for goodness' sake!" Penny grumbled. "Would you please just go to the podium so we can get on with the meeting?"

Bella's glare should've sliced Penny off at the knees. It didn't do a thing. Her sour expression didn't budge. But Bella did.

Thankfully.

"What on earth do you think you're doing?" I asked when she finally reached my side.

She tipped up her nose. "What I do every Saturday morning. Just like you."

I crossed my arms. "You know what I mean. Why did you bring *her* here?"

Bella glanced toward the back of the room. "I told you, Haley girl. I like Cissy. She wasn't doing anything this morning now that the brothers found a man nurse to care for their dad. I figured we could come to the meeting, shop for cat food afterward, and maybe catch some Court TV or *Police Files* at my place after that."

Swell. Wilmont's elderly female Batman and budding Robin planned to further feed their obsession.

Before I had a chance to say a thing, Bella's look took a calculating turn. "What's with you? Don't you want to find out more about Cissy and Darlene and the Weikert men? You don't really buy the cancer story, do you?"

She knows me. Too well. "Oh, all right. But I *won't* go anywhere for cat food, and I *won't* watch Court TV with the two of you and the cats."

"Fine, fine. Just have lunch with us. You gotta eat someplace, don't you?"

I rolled my eyes, gestured her back toward her guest, and then took up my gavel. I pummeled the top of the lectern. The room quieted. From that point on, the meeting unfolded normally. Well, normal if you consider Penny's indignant sniffs, snorts, and snuffles normal.

As the meeting drew to a close, dread sloshed around in my gut. I was going to lunch with Bella and her latest pal, the new heiress and possible murderer.

Turns out I had good reason to worry. We hit a nearby all-you-can-eat buffet place where I was the youngest patron by three centuries or more. Hidden among the various forms of mystery meat in the warming trays, I found small tubs of iceberg lettuce, carrot shreds, tomato wedges, and limp cucumber bits.

At least I knew what I was eating.

The conversation ran along the lines of cats and dogs. It turns out that Cissy is another cat person. The avowed dog lover in the threesome who didn't have much to contribute to their learned discussion shrank in her chair and munched on water and cellulose splotched with semisolid Thousand Island dressing.

After a time of praise for cats and their idiosyncrasies, Bella swung right into her PI bit.

"So what do you think of the Weikerts and Darlene's death?"

Cissy sighed. "I miss her so much. We were friends for years."

I made a mental note of the question she didn't answer.

"How many?" Bella asked.

"About twenty. Her boys were little, and my daughter had died years before. I had so much fun watching Darlene with them. She had them late and loved everything about motherhood. I did warn her she was going to regret all the spoiling. And she did soon enough."

I sat up, but Bella beat me to the punch.

"What made her regret it?" she asked.

Cissy squared her shoulders. "They never worked a day in their lives. At least, not until Darlene set up that mooch Tommy in his foreign car sales place, and I still don't know how much work he really does."

"Did she buy the showroom for Tommy?"

"At least she didn't go that far. All he owns is the clothes Darlene paid for him to buy so he wouldn't run around naked. She's paid the rent on that place and his apartment from the start. You'd think she'd learn after a while."

Hmm . . . Righteous indignation?

Bella picked up steam. "How about the cars? He's got a gaggle of them. They don't come cheap."

"Yes, they do. For him. She paid for those too."

Wilmont's pet detective leaned forward. "Bottom line, Cissy. Are you saying she shelled it out for him as if he still wore diapers? Is that the scoop?"

"That's the scoop."

Cissy's disgust with the deadbeat brothers sounded sincere. I don't know if I could stomach them either. So what was Tommy's problem? Had his landlord begun to drum him for late rent now that Darlene was dead? I couldn't forget his phone conversation at the showroom.

But Bella didn't give me a chance to ask again.

"If Mama still paid his bills," she said, "he'd want to keep her around, don't you think? Is he dumb enough to snuff her? Without her around, he's pancake-flat broke."

"Yes, he is." Cissy's satisfaction made her brown eyes livelier than I'd ever seen them. "But he never thought she'd cut him out of her will. She did it because she finally began to see the light. She felt she had to protect Jacob's future for the day the cancer took her."

She fell silent, and her grief seemed real and deep. I could relate. After Marge's murder, I struggled to get past the loss and pain.

"Maybe," Cissy continued after a moment or two, "Tommy made another one of his dirty deals recently, one for more than Darlene was willing to give him. And that might have led him to . . ."

"Ooh, baby! *One* of his dirty deals? Does he do that a lot? How much dirt does he"—Bella shuffled imaginary cards—"deal out?"

"He hung out with some shady characters. It felt like

every other week they came up with another 'sure thing.' But none of those 'sure things' ever worked out quite as Tommy said they would, and Darlene always bailed him out."

On the one hand, Tommy had a pretty strong motive. On the other, maybe not so much. And Larry knew about his brother's iffy ethics all along. Was that what Techno Whiz Kid had pulled up on the computer screen?

Bella barreled on, and I sat back. Who was I to mess with—I think—success?

"How 'bout that other kid?" she asked. "You know, the pocket-protector one."

Cissy snorted, the most unladylike sound I'd heard the plain but proper senior make. "He's another story. He works—all the time. Or so he says. But no one knows what he does. All Darlene could tell me was that it had something to do with very innovative, hush-hush computer stuff."

"So this one's not a bloodsucker leech?"

Good grief, Bella. How subtle can you get?

"I didn't say that." Cissy pursed her lips for a moment, then let out a slow breath. "No, this one begs and borrows too. But he calls it 'investments' in computer hardware. And he did bring the machines and strange gadgets for Darlene and Jacob to see. Not that they knew a thing about electronics, you know."

I figured Jacob didn't know much of anything by then—who knew how long the poor man had been suffering from Alzheimer's.

Bella didn't let up, even though Cissy seemed on the

up-and-up. "But this one pays his rent and food and junk, right?"

Cissy shrugged. "Who knows? Over the years Darlene gave him a lot of money. He could still be living off the latest sum."

"And when did he snooker that wad out of her?"

Bella does have a way with words.

Cissy paused and thought. "About a year ago. I figure he's probably due for another transfusion into the Larry-the-Bill-Gates-wannabe dream fund. A refusal might have made him mad enough."

"What's he need more for? How many computers can he want?"

Bella had a point. Where would Larry put more computers? And he wasn't sinking the cash into his house; the paint was peeling worse than a blonde with a sunburn. Clothes? He didn't dress for success.

"Larry says computers become obsolete the minute they leave the manufacturer's warehouse." Cissy looked uncertain. "I don't know much about electronics, so he could be right."

I'd heard it said a number of times. Living in Bill Gates's part of the country made even the staunchest of technophobes aware of certain realities.

Then Bella really kicked it up a notch.

"So where are you getting your regular fits of MGM?"

"Fits? MGM?" Cissy asked.

"Hey, I'm hip. That's what kids call druggies' daily helpings of their poison."

Maybe I'd just slip under the table. How could Bella flat out call Cissy, a woman who could quite possibly be as innocent and nice as she again seemed, a junkie?

With great dignity, Cissy said, "You must mean *fix*, Bella. And I'll have you know I'm no drug addict. I'm a retired nurse, a student of health sciences. I support research and development. And just you wait. One of these days everyone will line up for their routine HGH shot just like me."

Bella pushed her lips out. "Ooh, baby. Not me. No way, no how. You won't ever catch me shooting up with some voodoo juice cooked up who knows where by who knows who."

Again Cissy took offense. "It's produced at a research lab in Mexico, Bella, and Dr. Díaz is very well respected in the medical community. He knows what he's doing."

My head began to throb; the mental ping-pong game had everything to do with it.

Bella went in for the kill. "I bet he does. Do you?"

I cringed. Bella's antics had to stop. "What kind of question is that?"

She pounded the table. "The kind that gets real answers, Haley girl. If we want to get to the bottom of this, then someone's gotta do that kind of asking. I'm doing it 'cause you're just sitting on your butt watching lettuce wilt."

She was right. I had sat like a lump from the moment she'd taken up the reins of the conversation. Unfortunately, we hadn't learned a thing. Well, some. But not much. Not enough that I could take it to Lila and get anywhere with her.

"I think what Bella means," I ventured, "is that we don't understand why you're willing to risk your health on an unproven remedy."

"I want to do my part. I want to help those who are working to prove the value of HGH. I want to give people hope. I want . . . I want to help eliminate the threat of death."

The fear Larry had mentioned cast a shadow across her face. I reached out and covered her hand. "Why would you want to do that?"

Her fingers trembled. "Because it hurts so much to lose those you love."

"I'll buy that. I still miss my mother, and she's been gone a couple of years now. Also a friend who died after her. But I'm okay. I've moved into a new place in my life. Everyone does that after the loss doesn't sting so bad."

Her hand spasmed into a fist, and she looked away. "But don't you worry what she went through? How scared she must have been? Where she is now? How hopelessly lonely she must be?"

"Oh dear . . ." Bella's bulldog feistiness was gone.

I met her gaze. Cissy had no faith. What a sad way to live. I knew it too well.

"I don't worry about my mother," I said in a gentle voice. "I never have. I know where she is and who is at her side."

Cissy yanked her hand away. "How? How can you possibly know?"

"Because I know the one who holds our lives in his hand. And my mother knew him too. Today she's face-to-face with him, and all her pain and fears are gone. The God of heaven takes care of his own."

"Everyone's got a God story," Cissy said with a shrug. "I've never come across one that sounds right. There's the New Age guys who say you're your own god; there's the pagans who worship Egyptian deities and trees and rocks; and then there's the Muslims and Buddhists and Hindus and everything else in between. Everyone's got a story to tell."

"There is a difference," Bella said.

"What's that?" Cissy asked.

"Only one story tells about when God became a man and died on a cross for us—you too. None of the other stories hold water; they're missing the love, the sacrifice, that real, live, here-today-to-stay truth."

"You're talking about Jesus, and I know he taught good things. But all religions teach different versions of the same kind of thing. There's no difference there."

My heart broke at the bleakness in her voice. I remembered when I turned away from God's love. I'd felt so alone.

"The God of the Bible promises forever at his side," I said. "All we have to do is accept his Son's sacrifice on our behalf."

"That's what they teach," Cissy countered, "but it's too simple, too easy. You can be as horrible and criminal as you want, then one day say, 'Hallelujah! Thank you, Jesus,' and everything's okay. Besides, you can't know that any of it's true. There's nothing to show that God will do what he says he's going to do."

"That's faith, Cissy," Bella said. "It's like when you fly in a plane. You don't see anything holding that plastic and steel sausage full of people up in the air. But you do see them fly over your head all the time. So you take it on faith that your plane's going to fly too."

A sausage? Okay.

"There's physics and math to explain why planes fly," Cissy argued. "That's a world away from taking words written thousands of years ago as truth."

"Once you do accept that truth," I said, "God reveals himself to you, more each day. Take it from someone who walked away from him at the worst possible time of her life."

"I'm happy for you," she said. "But for me, I'd rather eliminate the reality of death."

I knew when to back down, but I also knew that Cissy had just found a home in my prayers. She needed God in her life. But she wasn't ready to meet him, so I returned to our original tack.

"You helped yourself to Darlene's HGH, didn't you?"

"I'm not proud of what I did," she answered. "But yes. I'm committed to the success of HGH research, and so I ordered twice as much serum as Darlene needed. We both took it. I know what I saw with my own two eyes."

"What did you see?"

"I saw Darlene get her color back. I saw her grow stronger, put back on some of the weight she'd lost, and I saw her become more like her old self again."

"And you're sure that MGM hormone did all that?"

Cissy smiled. "HGH, Bella."

"Same difference." There was no budging Bella once she made up her mind. "What about that stuff? Are you sure that's what made Darlene get better? Are you sure it wasn't the cancer going into recession? Or the chemo working?"

"Remission," Cissy corrected. "Yes, the oncologist did say the malignancy was gone, but Darlene went into remission before. She didn't rebound like this that other time, and that was earlier in the course of her disease. The only difference was the HGH."

I'd had about all I could take. I stood. "Cut it to the bare bone here, Cissy. Why are we still talking about Darlene's death? The woman had liver cancer. She was terminal. What's the deal?"

Her mellow brown gaze met mine. "It's all about what I saw. I'm sure the cancer didn't take her life. Someone killed Darlene."

I fell back onto my chair and just sat, too stunned to say another word. For once even Bella was speechless.

"So now there are three of you," Dutch said from behind my back. "I guess that old cliché is true: birds of a feather do flock together."

He pulled a chair from the empty table next to ours, swung it around, and straddled it at my side. "How do you do it, Haley? How do you work yourself up and convince yourself that a crime's been committed where nothing's happened? How do you sell the story? How do you live with the snoop you've become?"

"Hi, Dutch. Fancy seeing you here. To what do I owe this uncommon pleasure?"

"You, Haley. You're why I'm here. And it's a good thing too. Otherwise, you'd have sent these two women out to do your dirty work."

"I'd never do such a thing. You're . . . you're a . . . a . . . you're a jerk, Merrill. And I hope I never see you again."

My anger boiled so high that I ignored the chorus of gasps that followed me outside. I paid no attention to the flood of incoming senior citizens but marched right to my car, got in, and just plain old stewed.

How could he? That was the nastiest thing anyone had ever said to me. I wouldn't risk the safety of a pair of elderly women. I'd done everything I could to keep Bella away from the Weikert family. And I certainly had nothing to do with Cissy's suspicions. She came up with those all on her own.

Knuckles rapped on the roof of my car.

"Go away!"

"Wow, Haley. You sure know how to hurt a guy."

I groaned. "I don't have the energy for your games, Chris. Doesn't Lila keep you busy enough at the cop shop these days?"

My former classmate opened the car door. "Scoot over. Something's up with you, and I'm not just the goofball you remember from back in sixth grade."

"I hope not. You're a cop now, for goodness' sake."

"And a good one too. So good that I detect trouble in your paradise. Go ahead. Move over. Tell Uncle Chris all about it."

Too tired to argue, I moved. Chris sat behind the wheel.

"Do you want me to drive you home?" he asked after a couple of silent minutes.

"No. I'm sure you're busy. You don't have to babysit me."

"Trust me, Haley. Babysitting is the last thing on my mind when I think of you."

"Sure. You're busy cooking up ways to either torment me or lock me up."

"Not exactly."

The serious ring of his words made me glance sideways. What I saw on his face made me catch my breath. And scared me to bits.

"If you think about it," he said, "you can figure out I've had a crush on you since back in sixth grade. But sixth-grade males aren't what you'd call suave and debonair. You never gave me the time of day, not even in high school. So I burned off the pain of my heartbreak and unrequited love by thinking up ways to torment you."

"Give me a break! That pickup line's so lame, it limps."

"Did it work?"

I had to laugh. The mischief in his blue eyes was contagious. "I don't know. I've never thought of you as anything other than the tormentor you mentioned."

"How about you give me some different kind of thought now? Are you busy Friday night? A couple of guys on the force say that new Thai restaurant is really good. Do you like Thai?"

And just like that, I had to face the one thing I'd avoided for a long, long time. A real, live, walking, talking, breathing man had just asked me out. I hadn't gone on a date since . . . since that hideous night five years ago when my date raped me.

I met Chris's gaze. I saw more there than I expected. I saw understanding, compassion, caring, and admiration. I also saw uncertainty, the fear that I might say no.

Sincerity glowed in his gaze. I couldn't look away.

"You can trust me, Haley. You know you can. I would never do to you what that animal did. It's your choice, and I understand if you can't."

Tears filled my eyes. The tenderness in his voice moved me. Fear held me back.

Something wafted up from the fog of my past . . .

"Perfect love drives out fear . . ."

Oh, Lord . . . why did you let this happen? What am I going to say? What should I do?

As I sat in my car and prayed, a nugget from the Bible rang in my heart. *"So do not fear, for I am with you; do not be dismayed, for I am your God. I will strengthen you and help you; I will uphold you with my righteous right hand."*

Chris had asked me to trust him. I didn't think he had it in him to hurt anyone, but I had no way to know for sure. Only God knows the heart of any of his children. So this wasn't really about trusting Chris.

This moment, this possible date, was all about my love

of God, my trust in him. I thought back to what I'd told Cissy. And that's when I knew. I knew I had to put my money where my mouth was. Was I really ready to trust him, even in this?

Had I really come home to my heavenly Father? Dare I try and minister to Cissy, to help her face her fears, if I wasn't ready to take that step myself?

Oh, Father, help me. Give me strength, courage, faith. Hold me; keep me in your hand.

"Sure, Chris. Let's give it a try."

8

"How could I have done that?" I wailed later that night.

"What, Haley?" Tedd asked. "How could you have done what? Agree to go to dinner with an old friend from school? That doesn't sound all that strange or difficult to me."

Although her voice sounded scratchy over her cell phone, Tedd's point came across loud and clear.

"It would be normal if *I* were normal. But I'm not."

"Are you going to stay 'not normal' for the rest of your life?"

"I don't know."

"Are you saying you can't trust God to heal you? To maybe even restore some of what was stolen from you?"

I took a sharp breath. "But how can I know? How do *you* know a date with Chris is what God wants me to do?"

"That's faith, Haley. You take God on faith. You trust him to see you through even this."

Her words brought the crazy conversation with Cissy and Bella to mind. I'd tried to share my love for the Lord with Cissy, but now I faced a real test: I had to put that love into action. I had to live that trust before I could expect Cissy to see it in me.

It wasn't good enough to talk; I had to walk the walk.

My chuckle came out kind of choked. "Funny how God works sometimes."

"Why do you say that?"

"Listen, shrink lady. Are you anywhere near?"

"I was on my way home, but I pulled off when I saw your number on my phone. Are you home?"

"Want to stop by?"

"Sure. I'll be there in a couple of minutes."

Tedd arrived, and as usual, we had to allow for Midas to greet *his* guest. They played fetch with his favorite rope knot, and then Tedd rewarded him with a doggy cookie. He plunked down at her feet and stared up at her with an excess of adoration. He wanted more: more games and many, many, many more cookies.

But I needed to sort through an avalanche of jumbled feelings. And after I convinced Midas that no more cookies were to be had, we left the kitchen and went to the living room. Tedd sat in a corner of the white-slipcovered couch, and as usual, I chose my late mother's rocker. I told my therapist-turned-friend about Cissy's lunchtime grilling. When I'd brought her up to speed, she sat for a handful of silent minutes.

"What's your take?" she finally asked. "Do you still think Cissy killed her friend?"

"My head says she had the best motive of all—she inherits a good-size estate. But my heart? My heart tells me she didn't do it. If she did it, then why would she question the coroner's report? You'd think she'd be planning a party or a trip to Brazil for Carnaval."

Tedd took a minute to digest. "If I had to go by what I learned in criminal psychology as well as my clinical experience with a wide variety of minds, I'd have to say you're right. I don't think Cissy Grover killed Darlene."

"Cha-ching! Chalk one up for me. I did pretty good. And I didn't spend a bundle or half my life to become a shrink either. How'd you like that?"

"Ah . . . but you can't tell people what to do like I can, with my kind of authority."

I snorted. "Yeah right. I'd like to see you give me one single, solitary direction. Your style runs more along the lines of a dentist's drill: dig, dig, dig."

"Does SCUBA ring a bell?"

"That was a dare. That's different. You don't command."

"I make you think, and that's moved you from that dark pit where you were to this new, lighter place. That's what I'm trained to do. And with God's help, I'm going to see you come all the way out on the other side."

"Are *you* there?"

"Talk about dig, dig, dig."

I mimicked obeisance. "I learned from the best."

Tedd glanced at her laced hands. "I think I am there. And I won't tell you I've forgotten one second of the rape, but I turned the rage and pain into resolve to heal myself and help others heal. After a while of despair, I came to the Lord, and he's brought me here. I have to believe he's kept his promise."

"You're still not married."

"I've come close."

"Really? I didn't know that."

"You know, Haley? Sometimes I forget we haven't known each other all that long. And I do tend to keep much of myself inside."

"Wanna share?"

She laughed. "Okay. While protecting the names of the innocent, I will confess it took me years to get where I am today. I've had two serious dating relationships since the attack. One came very, very close to the altar. But in the end neither worked out."

"Because of you?"

Tedd picked up a vintage tapestry throw pillow and hugged it close "No. And not because of the guys either. There was love and companionship and passion, but either the timing was wrong, or the place didn't work, or the faith wasn't where it had to be for one or the other of us. Like I said, neither was right."

The question that burned in my heart was the hardest to ask. But I really had to know. "Did you worry all the time that they might . . . that they might turn and—"

"I understand. And no. Well, at first, when I didn't know either one very well, I'd get the occasional pang of fear, but I made myself keep my eyes on the cross. That's where I had to drop the past, the fear—everything—and not pick it up again."

"That's the hardest part."

"I won't argue there."

We both fell silent, each of us dealing with memories of horrible times and our trips back.

"So what are you going to do?" Tedd asked.

I took a deep breath. "I'm going to go."

"Good for you! I'll be praying for you."

"And I'm going to hold you to that promise, shrink lady."

"That's fine. You do that. And remember to enjoy yourself."

"You don't ask much, do you?"

She laughed again. "Make up your mind, will you? First you say I ask too many questions, and now you say I don't ask much. What's it going to be?"

I rolled my eyes. "Ever try to have fun with a six-foot-plus evil shadow hanging around?"

"Do tell."

My rocking picked up speed. "You should've heard Dutch. He showed up at the all-you-can-eat place and plunked down at my side. He called me a snoop and accused me of sending Bella and Cissy to do my, as he called it, dirty work. He meant detecting."

"I think he might have a teeny, tiny point somewhere in all that, Haley. Your curiosity is way too overdeveloped. It has landed you in trouble a time or two. It's what gave Bella the final push to get her PI license."

"That curiosity also solved two murders before innocent people—me included—were locked up for good."

"I grant you that, but your curiosity goes wild and lands you at the wrong place at the wrong time. That only serves to make matters worse for you."

"True, but my curiosity redeemed itself. It landed the killers where they belong: in jail."

"Is that what you're after here? Do you think someone killed Darlene Weikert and you need to bring them to justice?"

"Someone has to. You have to admit, too many scum are out there free to roam the earth."

"Is it your job to nab them?"

I shrugged and watched my grumpy dog collapse on the hooked floral rug in front of the fireplace.

Tedd didn't speak right away. Then, "Or is it a case of locking up those you can since the one who hurt you got away?"

I winced. She was right. The man who raped me got off with the equivalent of a slap on the hand. I can't stand to see anyone victimized; I know too well how it feels. And there is no greater victimization than murder.

"What can I say? I don't think Darlene's cancer caused her death. Yes, it would've killed her sooner or later, but someone wanted her gone bad enough to hurry things up. I want to know who and why. She was a really neat lady—you should know. Her sons took advantage of her all the time, but she loved them enough to help them over and over again. And the way she cared for Jacob . . . it couldn't have been easy. She had more patience than I'll ever have."

"I'm impressed. You saw her only once, and you have Darlene Weikert pegged to a T. How'd you do it?"

"Come on, Tedd. It doesn't take a genius to see character like hers."

"And you're offended by her potential murder."

"Everyone should be offended by murder."

"But not everyone chases killers."

"Not everyone's been raped."

She stiffened. "Wow."

"Sorry. That was kind of a dig, but it's how I feel."

"And it's what makes you tick these days, isn't it?"

"Not by itself. Faith and love have a lot to do with my get-up-and-go. I have faith in the Lord's love and his promise to heal. And I love Dad. I couldn't just shrivel up and die on him."

"Just as you can't let Lila and her officers do their jobs."

"If they did them, I'd feel differently."

"And have you told Dutch about all of this? What happened to you and how it made you the kind of person you are? He can't get into your head, you know."

I flinched. "That's a low blow, Tedd." The rocker could've won the Indy 500 at the speed I cranked it to. "Of course I haven't told Dutch any of this. I don't think I've ever put it into words before. Besides, what does Dutch have to do with anything?"

"My question was to make you think, not to have you answer. But since you did, I have to remind you that not so long ago you didn't want Dutch to be less than you hoped he was. I don't think you're as immune to him as you'd like."

I sputtered.

I shook my head.

I stood and went to the door. "It's late. I'm sure you're tired and want to get going—"

"Don't run away. And I don't mean from home. You know your feelings for Dutch push you out of your comfort zone. I knew sooner or later you'd panic at the thought of a date, but I always thought Dutch would be the guy."

I walked back to the rocker. "Why would you want me to date a man who thinks I'm so rotten?"

"I didn't say I wanted you to date him. I think *you* want to date him—but you can't admit it. Even to yourself."

Did I tell her now that I'd accepted the attraction I felt for him a while back? And that she was dead-on right?

Nah.

My soul had dropped its drawers long enough for one night. "Well, for what it's worth, I'm not going out with Dutch, and I'm not crazy about him right about now."

She chuckled. "Okay. I'll let you get away with it tonight. But you're going to have to face your feelings sooner or later. Just remember that Chris is a decent guy, and he doesn't deserve to be stuck in the hot seat between you and Dutch."

"Weren't we talking about the Weikerts?"

"Tell me about the Weikerts."

"I think the sons did it. But I have to prove Darlene died of something besides cancer. And since nothing else came up in the coroner's report, and no one bothered to run a toxicology screen, I have to find a way to get them to do it."

"You don't take on small challenges, do you?"

"If it's worth doing at all, then it's worth doing it all. And this time it's worth doing the complete autopsy, soup to nuts." I caught myself. "Yuck! That was ghoulish. Sorry. But you get what I mean. And it's a good thing Darlene's sons have dragged their feet on the funeral and she's not been buried yet. It'd be harder to get where we need to go if we had to exhume her body."

Tedd stood, picked up her cordovan leather briefcase, and went to the door. "I have to wonder if you didn't major in the wrong field."

"Whoa! Dad said the same thing."

"Maybe we're onto something."

"But you guys think Bella and her PI license are a crazy joke. I don't want to be lumped in with a nut like her."

"Why not? You're an awful lot alike."

"Hey! I'm all about the victim, and Bella's all about the boredom. She needs to get a life beyond those two maniacal cats."

"What if you turn matchmaker? Find her a romance, and maybe she'll settle down."

"Bella? A romance?" I couldn't see it. "Not in this life-time."

She opened the door. "Keep it in mind. Love can make people do all kinds of uncharacteristic things."

"Sounds like you speak from experience."

She winked. "I told you I struck out twice, didn't I? Now let me head on out. I didn't spend the day chatting up two elderly ladies and fending off good-looking males. I'm tired."

I groaned. "Don't remind me. I have paperwork up to my eyeballs, and I don't know when I'll get to it. I have this big job for this very picky shrink here in town. Her dumpy office needs a makeover in the worst way."

She laughed all the way to her car. I closed the door and leaned back against it. Dad was at a meeting. Midas was asleep. Tedd was gone.

It was just me and my thoughts, thoughts Tedd's questions had raked up. The questions didn't bother me. Not so much.

But the answers?

Those scared my mouth cotton dry.

The next morning I came too close for comfort to being late for the worship service. I blamed it all on Tedd. Questions and answers had buzzed in my head the whole night long.

I plopped into the aisle seat in the last pew and only then noticed my pew mate.

"What's the deal, Haley girl? Where you been? You're usually here before everyone but your daddy."

The first notes to "How Great Thou Art" filled the sanctuary.

"Bad night," I whispered.

Bella's blue eyes showed her concern. "I'll pray for you, honey. And I'm glad you're here now."

No matter how nutty she might be, Bella is still one of my favorite people in the world. I tipped my head sideways and laid it on her shoulder for a fraction of a heartbeat.

"I love you too," she murmured.

Then we both joined the congregation's song of praise.

Little by little my nerves began to uncoil. I sat back to wait for Dad's sermon. And I waited. As did the congregation.

The seconds morphed into minutes, and I tensed up again. If Bella had been worried by my lateness, I could just imagine what Dad's would do to her.

Finally he came across the chancel to the pulpit, his gait uneven, a hand at his waist. Had he fallen and hurt himself? What had he been doing while I fought my battle with the bedsheets?

Guilt struck, even though I knew accidents happen all the time. I caught my bottom lip between my teeth, asked forgiveness, and prayed for Dad.

He started his sermon and before long stepped out from behind the pulpit. He never can stay put while he delivers the message and always walks back and forth before the altar table.

But no sooner did he take three steps than he backed up, his hand again at his waist. At the pulpit, he stared down where he always puts his notes, but he didn't continue with the message. His frown deepened. He seemed to struggle, to try to find the right words.

What was wrong?

Had he left his notes at home?

He rarely relies on them. I can't remember the last time he needed a prompt, but he always brings them just in case. Today I couldn't figure out what was going on. And it worried me.

I prayed harder.

Dad spoke again but didn't quite pick up where he'd left off, and he hesitated every so many phrases. It didn't go unnoticed in the pews. A few people traded glances. Some shrugged. Others seemed oblivious. One older gentleman, who shall remain nameless, let out a snore.

Then Dad began to pace again. And again, after he took a couple of steps, he grabbed at his waist and hurried to the shelter of the pulpit. It took him a bit longer to fumble his way back into his sermon. My concern continued to grow.

I prayed even more.

I watched the same pattern repeat itself over and over until he wrapped it all up. He gave the final blessing, nodded to the choir, and grabbed the sides of the pulpit instead of coming down the aisle to stand and greet the worshipers at the church's front door—what he always does.

When I went to leave the pew, Bella caught my hand.

"Wait," she whispered. "Let them go. You don't want to scare anyone any more than they already are."

Nothing much got past Bella. "You're right. Dad wouldn't want me to make a fuss." I stared at my father, but he didn't move a muscle. "What do you think is going on?"

"Beats me, Haley girl. But we're going to figure it out as soon as this place empties."

Most of the congregants left, their plans for the afternoon set. A few, mostly church board members, lingered at the door. Bella elbowed me, then jerked her head in their direction.

I smiled, nodded, and waved. After a couple more nods

and waves, they left too. That's when Bella and I rushed forward.

"Dad!"

"Hale, what's up? What'd you think you were doing up here?"

Our questions seemed to startle Dad. He narrowed his gaze, glanced down at the pulpit, shook his head, then turned to me. "Haley?"

"Yes, Dad. Of course, it's me. What's wrong? Do you feel sick?"

He patted himself, his chest, his front pockets, the back ones as well, then shook his head. "No, I don't think so."

"Then what's going on?"

"I can't remember . . ." He grabbed for his waist again. "Haley? Where's my belt?"

"Do you mean to tell me you aren't wearing one? That's what all the weird stuff up here was about? Your pants falling down?"

"That's it. But I know I took the belt off the hook on the closet door. I thought I put it on . . ."

A quick check under his jacket showed me empty belt loops on his pants. "What about your notes? It seemed to me you didn't have them."

Bella weighed in. "I figure he forgot the belt, forgot the notes, and almost lost his pants. What a morning, Pastor Hale!"

She got a smile out of him. I let out my breath.

Then he said, "I don't have my notes. I know I wrote them, but . . . I don't have them now."

The absentmindedness was growing worse by the day. "Okay, Dad. Let's go home and find your stuff."

When we got to the manse, the belt and the notes were spread out on his bed, where he'd probably put them when he started to dress.

Maybe it was time for a checkup. I had to make sure to set up an appointment for him with Dr. Cowan. I'd call first thing Monday morning.

Today, however, I too had plans. I was going to the Weikert home. I had questions for Jacob.

I prayed he'd be lucid enough to understand.

I got to the Weikerts' at the same time Cissy did. "Hi there!"

"Haley! I didn't expect to find you here."

"After our conversation yesterday, I knew I had to do something. I've thought from the start that there's more to Darlene's death than her disease. I just have to find a way to prove it."

"Prove it? Isn't that a job for the police?"

"It should be." I spread my arms and turned 360 degrees. "What do you see them doing?"

She made a face. "There's just the two of us here."

"And Jacob inside."

"There's the new nurse Tommy and Larry hired. They didn't want me near Jacob. They had the gall to say I would kill him to get my hands on the rest of Darlene's money."

I turned to the house. I didn't want her to see me blush. I'd thought so too. But now I was pretty sure Jacob had always been safe in Cissy's care. I didn't know if I could say the same about the new nurse.

"It can't hurt to visit Jacob, can it?"

"What a splendid idea! We really should see how my replacement is doing."

A burly middle-aged man opened the door when we rang. "Yes?"

"Hi!" I nearly choked at my perkiness. "We're friends of the family and stopped by to see how Jacob is today."

The man's heavy brow furrowed. "He's the same as always. Why wouldn't he be?"

"Oh, that's not what I meant. We'd like to visit awhile."

"He's not well enough for that. He's too confused."

"We know." Cissy extended her right hand. "I'm Cecelia Sparks, longtime friend. And you're . . . ?"

Sparks? What was that about?

He shook her hand. "Dave Williams, Jacob's new nurse. I just started this week."

Cissy smiled. "I'm so glad to see he has someone to lean on. His disease is so devastating."

They discussed the horrors of Alzheimer's for a few minutes, then Cissy brought the conversation back to Jacob and our hoped-for visit.

"We care for him," she said, her voice warm and sincere. "That doesn't change just because he's sick. And we won't stay long. Just enough to say hello, maybe play a game of checkers or two. He loves checkers."

We must not have looked like mass murderers or terrorists, and the Brothers Brat must not have provided Dave with a picture of their dreaded Cissy, because he led us inside. Jacob sat in the faded parlor, the antique French bergère chair dwarfed by his bulk.

"Jacob!" Cissy said, her voice cheerful and a touch loud. "How are you?"

He turned toward us, a vacant look on his face.

She pulled a matching chair to his side, sat, and leaned close. "It's Cissy. Want to play checkers?"

"Checkers?"

"Oh my, yes! You love checkers."

"I do?"

"Mm-hmm. You always beat me too."

A trace of a smile curved his lips. "And Dari?"

Cissy breathed in hard. "Oh dear. No, Dari won't be playing with us today. But this is my friend Haley. She wants to play. Will you let her join us?"

"Haley?"

That was my cue. "Hi, Jacob. We met before. On your beautiful front porch."

"Teddie?"

Cissy smiled. "Good, Jacob! You remembered Tedd. Haley knows her too. Now let's play."

Cissy pulled out a checkerboard and wooden pieces from the bottom drawer of a chest by the window. She spread the game out on the coffee table, and we started to play. Jacob moved pieces at Cissy's direction but didn't remember what he'd done only seconds later.

Every so often he looked up at me. "Dari?"

Cissy answered that his wife wasn't home, that I'd come

to see him. And we played on. Finally, when my heart was about to break at the sight of a grown man trapped in his still vigorous body by his ravaged mind, I turned to Cissy.

"We have to find out what happened. We owe it to Darlene and to him."

"What should we do?"

"We have to revisit that autopsy. We have to ask for a toxicology screen."

"Can we do it?"

"I think so."

"How do we go about it?"

I prayed my trust wasn't misplaced. "You are the executrix of the estate, right?"

She nodded.

"And in spite of what the sons did—replace you with Dave—you're Jacob's legal guardian, aren't you?"

"I am. I don't know why Darlene did things the way she did, but I know she trusted me with Jacob. She knew I'd never waste her money and that I'd take good care of him when she wasn't with us anymore."

"Then the best thing to do is approach this from the angle of protection for Jacob. If someone killed Darlene for her money, then he could be next."

I held my breath. Her response would say a lot.

She passed my test. The color leached from her face. "Oh, Haley. We have to hurry. We can't let anyone hurt him. Poor man. It's bad enough that the disease has done this to him and that Darlene's gone now, but for someone to kill him? For money?"

Her fingers trembled when I clasped them. Either she was innocent or the Sissy Spaceks and Nicole Kidmans of Hollywood had a lot to fear when Oscar time rolled around again.

"We have to do this for your sake too. You're in the way of anyone with an eye on the money."

She *hmphed*. "As long as the kids don't squander the money while their father needs it, I couldn't care less. Whoever wants it can have it. I'll give up my claim—but not before I take care of Jacob to the end."

Her fierceness came as a surprise, especially in contrast with her small frame, her bland face, her quiet voice. She angered big.

"I don't want you killed either," I said. "So we have to get that tox screen. We can't let up until we get what we need."

Cissy stood and held herself tall. "Count me in. Just tell me what I have to do."

"It won't be easy," I warned. "We have to convince a hardheaded homicide detective that there's more here than she thinks. We're going to have to spar with a pro."

I headed for the front door. "Dave? We're on our way. Thanks for the time you gave us with Jacob."

The big man came out from the rear of the house. "It's good for him to see people. And I haven't seen Tom or Larry since they hired me. When do you think you can come back?"

Cissy made arrangements to return in a few days, and then we left. Once we stood on the sidewalk, I turned to my companion and said, "Sparks, Cissy? Where'd you come up with that name?"

"It's my maiden name. I doubt Tommy or Larry know it. But I do know they'd object if Dave told them I'd been by."

"You don't think they'll wonder who Cecelia Sparks is?"

"Let them wonder. We had to do it, didn't we?"

"Yes, we did. And sometimes, Cissy, you just have to follow your gut. This is one of those times. And it's also time to go. There's a detective at the Wilmont PD we have to bring on board."

I prayed Lila would listen—listen and agree.

We would need more than just my own prayers on this one. You never know what it will take to sway Lila. I took a chance and put Bella on the job. She started up the Wilmont River Church's prayer chain.

Cissy and I drove straight to the cop shop.

Bella would meet us, bring up the rear. My prayer request had incited questions, and those questions aroused our favorite pet detective's curiosity. Just try to keep Bella away. Try it.

Prayer? Yeah, we needed prayer. Lots.

9

You never can tell with Lila. This time she just about shocked the socks off me—not that I wear socks with my Birks.

"I figured you'd get around to this sooner or later," she said once Cissy and I had laid out what we knew. "We can't refuse the family's request, or in this case, that of the executrix of the estate. If Mrs. Grover signs the necessary documents, a forensic pathologist will run a toxicology screen on the remains."

I'd come loaded for proverbial bear; I'd found an educated kitty cat instead. But I'd gotten what I wanted. And we would soon have the answers we needed.

Waiting wouldn't be easy, not for someone who lacks all patience. But I didn't have a choice. The tests would take a few days.

And I did have to work on Tedd's office. Not to mention the tons of paperwork stacked on my desk at the auction house. It was there, at my office in the warehouse, on Wednesday, that I got Bella's phone call.

"Haley? I got a problem."

"Only one?"

"This is no joke. I need your help."

She sounded serious, but in the background I could hear the familiar and fearsome wails and snarls of her two cats. "How much trouble are you and the beasts in?"

"Depends on what you call trouble."

What were the chances that whatever had Bella in an uproar wouldn't strike me as trouble? "Give it a whirl and tell me what's up. I'll tell you if I call it trouble."

"My car broke down."

"Call AAA."

Dead silence. Except the cats.

Bella has a special talent; I can always count on her to test my lousy excuse for patience. "Did you hear me? Why'd you call me instead of the auto club?"

"Um . . . they won't come to where I am."

"What? They're everywhere. They even offer some international services. What do you mean, they won't come to where you are?" A horrible possibility hit me then. "Please tell me you didn't leave the country."

"Well . . . it's like this. I . . . ah . . . took a little trip and wound up all turned around. Now my car's broke down, and they don't have a local auto club all that close to here."

"Bella, where are you?"

A fantastically loud howl made me strain to hear her response. I thought she said something about a desert. But that made no sense. Even if it was Bella on the phone.

"Come again? Your darling fur wad yowled over you."

"Now, Haley. It's a crying shame how you hurt Bali's feelings all the time. You know how sensitive she is."

Like sandpaper, but that wasn't the point right then. "We can talk about the cats later. Where are you?"

"I'm not exactly sure, and that's why AAA wouldn't send anyone after me. It's kinda lonely out here."

Now I began to worry. "Out where?"

"In the desert."

Last time I checked, the nearest desertlike terrain was way on the other side of Washington State, off to the north-east. I live on the coast, way in the west. Bella's house is right across the street from the manse.

"Are you speaking figuratively?"

"Watch it, Haley girl! I'm touchy about my weight gain."

Weight gain? Oh! "Figuratively." Good grief!

I tried again. "Are you talking sand and cactus, no water, and scorpions, or are you struggling with a different kind of problem? Spiritual, maybe?"

"Didn't I already tell you I got a problem? I'm in the desert—yep, it's drier'n Penny Harham's roast chicken out here."

"What are you doing there? And where?"

"Somewhere in Oregon."

"Oregon! Bella. Answer my question. Please. Why are you in Oregon?"

"It's not like I planned to wind up here. My car just pooped out on me."

Even though I knew the answer, I had to ask. "So what do you want me to do about it?"

"Come and get me."

"And how am I supposed to do that if even AAA can't figure out where you are?"

The silence grew. This time not even the cats disturbed it. Finally she said, "I'm kinda scared, Haley girl. I just gave the Balis my last bottle of water. And it's hot."

I'm not so hot with directions; let's just call me directionally impaired. And Bella had no clue where she was. But, as it turned out, she did know where she'd been before she took her wrong turn and where she was supposed to have wound up. Sadly, the two didn't match up.

"Look," I said when she finished her labyrinthine commentary on her roundabout journey to nowhere. "I'm not going out there. I'll never find you, and then we'll both turn into Georgia O'Keefe artwork—only not the flower kind, and not so much admired."

"What am I going to do?"

I could almost touch her fear. "Give me a chance to call someone. Maybe Lila can contact a cop shop in Oregon and they can figure out where you are. We'll get you back home one way or another."

"Okay." She didn't sound reassured. "But just make sure you get me home the one way. I don't think I'd like the 'another.' Thanks for making me get this dopey cell phone, Haley girl. I'd be well on the way to roadkill if you hadn't."

"Roadkill?" My voice could've shattered crystal. "Did a car hit you?"

"No. But I might've died on the side of the road, me and the Balis. So thanks."

Phew! "No problem, Bella. Now let me get Lila and the Smurfs on the job, okay?"

When we hung up, I realized I hadn't wormed out of her the answer to my other question. Why'd she go to Oregon, anyway?

As Ricky Ricardo used to tell Lucy, Bella had some splainin' to do.

"You did *what*?"

Bella squirmed in the Honda's passenger seat later that evening. "I went to check out that Dr. Díaz dude."

"You went to Mexico? And wound up in southeast Oregon? And here I thought I had trouble with directions."

"I started out for Tijuana, okay? But I only got so far as someplace near Portland."

I turned onto Puget Way, headed for the manse via Bella's place. The wails and hisses in the backseat made me desperate to dump out the box of furious felines. Maybe then I could concentrate on Bella's story and decipher what had happened.

"Let's try this again," I said. "Why did you feel the need to check out Darlene's Mexican doc? Tijuana's an awfully long way from Wilmont."

"It's a no-brainer. Someone's gotta see what he's up to. Fifty grand, and who knows how much more for his juju juice, is a lot of dough for Darlene to shell out."

Once in Bella's driveway, I let the Honda idle. "And you're the self-appointed looker-into."

"I'm the PI."

The hisses from the back picked up steam. "A good PI would figure out there won't be much left in that box but hamburger and lint soon. Let's get them loose."

She gave me a "Haley knows nothing" look. "That's how kitty cats play. Haven't you seen dogs? They snap and nip at each other's throats all the time."

Those shrieks sounded more painful than playful to me. "If you say so. And since you say you're the investigator, how about sharing what you learned about the Mexican doc?"

"Which one?"

I blinked. "You lost me. What do you mean, which one? There's more than one Mexican doctor involved?"

"Isn't your buddy Tedd Mexican?"

I clutched the steering wheel to keep from pulling my hair out. "You usually drive me nuts with too much information, but this time you'd better shell out the data before I go ballistic. Tedd's not exactly the same as the south-of-the-border guy, okay?"

"Chill, Haley. My goodness, dear. You're going to wind up with hibernation. That's not good for you. It could give you a stroke."

"Hypertension. Hibernation's what bears—never mind! And you're the one who shoots my blood pressure to the outer limits of the galaxy. Cut the cutesy clue-drop and tell it to me straight. What have you been up to?"

"I went to Mexico to check out the dope doctor but stopped in Oregon. I needed gas—you know how much it costs to fill the Caddy's tank these days? Whoo-eee! I remember when a gallon of gas was only fifty cents—"

"The doctor, Bella. What about him? We can discuss the decline of the economy later."

"All right already. I went south, bought gas, got hungry, and because I'm a lady all alone, I went to the restaurant at a nice hotel just outside Portland. Turns out, they were having a doctor's symphonium there. Place was packed."

By now the ruckus in the back was such that even Bella'd had enough. She got out of the car, retrieved the cardboard carton Chris had found in the dumpster behind the cop shop, and lugged it to her front door.

I had no choice but to follow—that is, if I wanted answers.

Once inside her mauve and lace and froufrou tchotchke-filled parlor, Bella released the hounds . . . well, right idea, wrong critter. At any rate, Bali H'ai and Faux Bali exploded from that putrid box like a high-fuzz pair of milkweed pods, and I experienced a similar allergic reaction to them.

Both turned on me, fur like bristle brushes, fangs bared, feral hisses louder than the warning in my brain that screamed, "Run!"

"Keep them away," I warned their owner.

"Get a grip," she said. "C'mon, girls. Mama's got din din."

Would you believe they listened? Who'd a thunk?

Silence reigned. An electric can opener whirred. The faint
tang of spoiled fish wafted forth. After that the triumphant
owner returned, and we both sat in aggressively floral Victorian reproduction furnishings, me in a chair, Bella on a
fainting couch.

"Gotta tell you, Bella. I never thought I'd see the day. But
you do know your maniacs. I give you a lot of credit."

"You're such a dog person. And in these days of equal
rights too. You oughta be ashamed, Haley girl. Discrimi-
nation's not cool."

"Uh . . . yeah. Well, are you going to tell me what happened in Oregon? How you . . . oh so coincidentally made
it to a medical symposium at a Portland hotel?"

"I made a couple of calls before I decided to take my
trip."

"Did you call the doctor's office? Tip them off that you
were about to chase the guy down?"

She smirked. "They can follow Martha Stewart all they
want."

"You told them you were the domestic diva?"

"Why not? All's I cared about was finding the quack. I
said it so I didn't have to tell them who I really am. Besides,
the girl I talked to didn't speak much English. She probably
doesn't know the diva. That's why I earned my PI license,
you know. I know how to cover my tracks. Anyway, I figured out where he was, and I headed south."

"To Portland. But how does the desert relate? Portland's
on the Washington border. The Oregon desert's down south
and near Idaho."

"I told you I got turned around."

"That's a lot of turning around you did."

"I heard 'em say something about going to Bend."

"Bend?"

"I took off," she said. "I figured I'd head them off, you know. Get there and see what was what. But I didn't even see Bend—at least, not Bend, Oregon. I saw lots of bends in the road though. D'you figure that's why they call the place that?"

She made me dizzy. Before I could find footing again, I had to establish a couple of facts. "Who did you hear?"

"The doctors."

"Which doctors?"

"One had a tag that read 'Roberto Díaz.' That's the dope dude from Tijuana, isn't it? And that was the symphonium he went to, wasn't it?"

"It could be any of a zillion doctors. That's not an uncommon name in Spanish."

"Yeah, but they were talking about the MGM."

I let it go. "And they said they were going to Bend, Oregon?"

"Well, I heard them say something about going to Bend. I just figured since we were in Oregon, that's what they meant. But they also said plenty about money. They want a lot of dough, those two."

Bend? A lot of dough?

In the same situation, I wouldn't have thought Bend, Oregon. I would've thought bent rules and regs. Then I thought of something.

"Did you happen to catch the subject of the symposium?"

"Didn't make much sense to me. These two were talking juju juice. The other docs were talking depression."

"Was it a mental health conference?"

"Maybe. I just know what I heard."

Mental health . . . Alzheimer's . . . HGH. Had Cissy been dosing Jacob as well as Darlene and herself?

I got up. "Well, Bella. At least you're home now. It might be a good idea to skip the road trips for a while. And the snooping? Leave it to Lila and the Smurfs. That's who can really follow the info and catch the killers."

A grumpy neighbor is way better than a desiccated one. On the other hand, it did look as though Bella had tracked down the right Roberto Díaz. The one who'd fed Darlene the HGH and borrowed fifty grand from her.

Time to let my fingers do some waltzing on computer keys.

After a couple of hours on the Web, I had a pretty good idea what Dr. Díaz wanted to do with HGH. And it wasn't as scary as what Cissy wanted. But it wasn't regular medicine either.

I called the good doctor's office the next day. For a possible appointment.

"Dr. Díaz no in office this week."

"Really? When will he be back?"

"Monday."

"Is he on vacation?"

The receptionist giggled. "No. He go conference business."

I had all the corroboration I needed. Bella had done well. Well, her research was right on, even if the wild goose chase through Oregon went way off.

I had more questions for the giggly girl. "Does he travel a lot? I mean, if I start treatment with him, will I have trouble seeing him because he's gone so much?"

"*Sí*, he travel. *Pero* he here too. People come all the time to office. *Pero* he travel for business, *sí*."

"Does he ever come to Seattle?"

"How you know?"

I don't know what threw me off the most, the receptionist's surprise at my question or that Dr. Díaz frequented Seattle.

Since it's always best to stick to the truth, I said, "I didn't know. I wondered because that's where I'm from. Does he see patients while he's here?"

"No many."

"But some, then?"

"Yes. Old patients . . . no, no. No old like many year old, *pero* old like lots of years his patient."

"Ah . . . I see. Will he be in Seattle again soon? I mean, the appointment you gave me isn't for three months, and if he travels my way, I'd like to at least meet him. I'd pay for the consultation, you understand."

She fell silent, then with clear reluctance said, "He in Seattle tomorrow. But he busy with business. I don't know . . ."

I asked her to go ahead and try to set up an appointment even though I held out little hope for a meeting. And I'd never even given a thought to keeping the appointment I'd used as an excuse to pump the girl for information. But then an idea began to congeal in a dark corner of my mind, so I said good-bye. I sat and doodled a while on my otherwise blank notepad.

There was no way to ignore fifty grand.

I dialed a local number. "Hi, Cissy. I've a question for you. Didn't you say the bank was in the process of arranging repayment of Dr. Díaz's loan? Or did I misunderstand? Did he pay back what Darlene loaned him?"

"Are you trying to stir up trouble for Dr. Díaz?"

"No. I'm just curious about the money. He could be a fabulous physician and a genius whose research brings about a breakthrough, but he could also be a killer if he can't come up with the dollars he needs for his work any other way. Darlene's dead. She left you in charge of Jacob and the money. Jacob suffers from a terminal disease. You support Dr. Díaz's research. What's to keep him from getting you to change your will and then coming after Jacob and you?"

Her response came in a tight voice. "The bank is in charge of the loan. I have a meeting in the morning with Darlene's lawyer to notarize the papers on the paid loan. Dr. Díaz has just received funding for his research from a European pharmaceutical company. He didn't need to kill Darlene, just like he doesn't need to kill Jacob or me."

A lot was happening tomorrow.

I was going to be a busy bee in the morning. I hoped the law firm had at least one chair in an inconspicuous corner. I wanted a look at this Dr. Díaz guy. No matter how much loan he'd come to repay.

Who knew where this money really came from? Who knew what Dr. Dope's game really was?

There was little to see at the offices of Warner, Mundy, Sears, and Rutt. Little besides the Mexican doctor's good looks, that is. Dr. Díaz was younger than I expected, in his midthirties, well dressed, great smile. Smooth. Like buttah! I could see why he had captivated Cissy and Darlene.

But he seemed to have followed through on the expected repayment. And Cissy had showed up with a loan officer from the Bank of Wilmont ten minutes before the doctor walked in. It looked to me like a cordial, even warm, meeting.

I left. There was nothing for me to see.

And then it was Friday. The dreaded day. But I couldn't ignore my looming date any longer. Chris would be here to pick me up at six thirty. To keep my mind off my darker fears, I ransacked my closet for decent clothes for the evening.

Since I hadn't dated in over five years, I found nothing I considered suitable. But I also refused to make such a big deal of the event as to spend hours in a mall.

When my room looked like the site of a tornado touch-down, I finally settled on a soft cream shirt and a tone-on-tone cream, bias-cut, long satin skirt. Then my nerves had me dressed and ready by five forty-five. Midas trotted up, gave me his intense brown stare, and walked away. Even he could tell I was too freaked to play.

"Arrghh!" This wasn't good. But I knew a good way to banish anxiety. With a glance at the clock, I headed for my chaise longue, my Bible, and time with my Lord.

By the time the doorbell rang, I thought I was ready to face Chris. But the Chris in our living room wasn't the Chris from my sixth-grade class. He wasn't the Chris in cop shop Smurf blues either. This Chris was an attractive blond man, dressed well if casually, with a smile that said he liked what he saw.

Hordes of butterflies filled my middle, and my palms grew damp. I prayed he wouldn't notice my nerves.

He seemed oblivious. "Ready?"

No! "Yes. Let's go."

He carried the conversation on the drive to the restaurant. He started out with a handful of funny cop stories, then followed those with a detailed retelling of his *Keystone Kops* efforts at a snowboarding park last winter.

When I quit laughing, I said, "That's because you're a surfer boy at heart. Come on. Tell the truth. Don't you just have this great big craving for a board and a wave? With your blond hair and that tan, you'd fit on any California beach."

He held up his hands as if to fend off the idea. "Don't blame me for my mom's Scandinavian genes. I've never even been to California. I'd be lost without the rain."

"Speaking of lost . . ." I told him about Bella, the Balis, and Bend.

We laughed—again—and I realized how many laughs we'd shared, more than I'd had in ages. That finally put me at ease.

The conversation flowed; my noodles and chicken, rich with Asian herbs and peanut sauce, were amazing; and I couldn't believe how much fun we had together.

That is, I had fun until my evil shadow walked in.

Lord? How could you let Dutch choose this restaurant this night?

Yeah, sure. It was a great new eatery, and it got a great deal of good buzz, but honestly. Was there nowhere I could go without tripping over the guy?

I shrank deeper into the booth and hoped he didn't see me, hoped Chris didn't see me trying to disappear— Houdini I am not. I wasn't so paranoid to think Dutch had followed me, but I could've and should've saved myself the effort of trying to hide. At least where Chris was concerned. He noticed Dutch moments after I did.

"Isn't that your partner over there?"

"Partner?" I squeaked. "Are you nuts? He's like bad wallpaper on my back—I can't scrape him off."

"I thought you two worked together."

"We've had to work together because we were both hired for the same three jobs. Unfortunately, dead bodies turned up at each of those jobs."

"Something like a Typhoid Mary syndrome?"

"Something like a contractor plague, if you ask me."

"But he was innocent, as innocent as you."

I sighed. "That's why he's still on the loose, free to torment me daily."

Chris sat back and looked at me. "You're kind of intense, Haley. Maybe you're driving him nuts too. Especially with your Sherlock Holmes impersonation."

"Low blow, Smurf man! I had no choice—"

"Smurf man? I'm not blue. What's that all about?"

I shrugged. "It seemed to fit back when Marge was killed. You know, the blue uniform."

"Wrong shade of blue, and you'd better not even think you can get away with calling Lila Papa Smurf."

That made me laugh again. "Blue is blue. But no. Not her. She's not Papa Smurf. She's the karate chop cop."

Chris choked on his mouthful of tea. After he swallowed, he mimed zipping his lips.

I winked. "Not a word, huh? She doesn't like it."

"I'd like to keep my job."

Then we talked about his job. He spoke of his dedication with passion and energy. He was smart, funny, attractive. He did noble work, and he clearly liked me. But something wasn't there.

I liked him, but as the friend he always should have been. There was something missing, a certain spark I didn't feel while in his company.

I sighed and looked toward the front of the room. There sat what was missing. As I looked, he must have sensed my gaze, because he raised his head, noticed me, tightened his jaw, and stared back. I sat motionless, silent. I let the realization soak in. Moments passed.

Then, beyond Dutch, a man and a woman entered the restaurant.

A shudder ran through me.

I froze.

When I finally moved, I reached across the table and grabbed Chris's hand. "Look."

I couldn't believe it. The woman I knew. The man, not at all. Not personally.

But it shocked me to see Tedd enter the restaurant on Dr. Roberto Díaz's arm. My stomach flipped. I felt not so good. There were a million reasons to doubt the man's innocence, even when I didn't know him. And now I had to connect him to Tedd.

My friend.

My therapist.

I didn't have to connect them; the connection was there, twenty-five feet away from me. Both of them were doctors. Both had treated Darlene Weikert. Could one be involved in her death? Could both?

Dear God, no!

10

I couldn't say what bothered me most, but between the mind-meld eye lock with Dutch and the sight of Tedd on Dr. Dope's arm, my evening was ruined.

Chris noticed. He sighed. "Ready to go?"

I nodded.

He held out his hand to help me out of the plush booth. "Interesting evening," he murmured.

"More like interesting patrons at this joint," I countered under my breath.

He chuckled. "Do you count us in that interesting crew?"

"We can't escape. We're all part of the Weikert case."

"I don't think there is a Weikert case, Haley. It's all in your overactive imagination."

"Let's see how overactive my imagination is when I hand you the killer on a silver platter."

"No peanut sauce, please."

"I'm going to do you a favor and ignore that supergross

comment." As I ignored away, I headed for the doctors' table.

"Aw, Haley, no. Come on . . ."

Chris's wail didn't slow me a bit. At tableside, I plastered on the best smile I could dredge up. "Fancy meeting you here, Tedd. But I guess this is *the* place these days. Never know who you're going to find when you come to eat."

The tint of deep rose beneath the caramel skin on her cheekbones revealed my therapist's discomfort. "Hi, Haley. Yes, I've heard great things about the food here. I figured we ought to see if it lives up to the raves."

"Oh, the food's great. I'll hold off my verdict on the patronage though. At least for a while."

Her blush deepened. "Let me introduce you to Dr. Roberto Díaz, from Tijuana. He's here on business. We've known each other for some time now."

I faced Dr. Dope. "Hi. I'm Haley Farrell. Welcome to my part of the world."

He stood, gave me his megawatt charmer smile, and clasped my hand in both of his. "The pleasure is all mine, Ms. Farrell." His voice bore the faintest trace of an accent. "Seattle is one of my favorite cities. Its people are some of the friendliest I've ever met."

His eyes slanted toward Tedd with his last words. I followed his gaze and noted my shrink's ever-greater discomfort. Swell. It looked like there was more than just business between these two. And one was a suspect in Darlene's death.

Too bad.

"We share—or maybe *shared* is the better word—another acquaintance, Dr. Díaz. I understand you treated Darlene Weikert with an unconventional serum."

His jaw tightened, and he sat. Without an invitation I pulled out one of the two empty chairs at the table. Behind me, Chris groaned. Tedd had no choice. She waved him to the last empty seat.

Once we'd all settled, I zoomed back in on Dr. Díaz. "How can that hormone, something that's not proven to treat diseases like cancer, help a woman close to the end of her life expectancy?"

Dr. Díaz leaned forward, his expression intense. "The HGH isn't a specific treatment for the malignancy, Ms. Farrell—"

"Call me Haley. Everyone else does."

He dipped his head. "Haley, the HGH—human growth hormone—promotes tissue repair and cell regeneration in bones, muscles, and vital organs and supports the immune system so that it can better fight infection and disease. When humans age, their levels of HGH drop to a fraction of those produced during youth. I'm sure you can see the connection for someone battling a terminal disease."

His lecture recapped what I'd learned on the Internet. "Forgive me, Doctor, but your last statement shot my skepticism right out into stratospheric orbit. If this HGH is as good as you say, then why doesn't every doctor have every patient pop it like an M&M?"

"It is a serum, not a pill. There is no popping. And the research is fairly new. Some of the best studies were conducted in the '90s. It often takes many in the medical community much longer than it should to accept new therapies."

"How well has this stuff been tested?"

"Consider this: we've used it on children with poor growth curves for decades. It can't be that harmful if we give it with good results to our most vulnerable patients."

"Yes, but those kids' bodies don't have the HGH they should have for them to grow normally. Now you're talking grown-ups. There's not a whole lot of growing going on. It seems to me, if the production goes down with age, then there has to be a good, natural reason for the drop."

"It declines because our bodies begin to wear out and can't make as much as they once could. Supplementation could prevent that wearing out process to a great degree."

"I see you're of the chicken-before-the-egg mentality, but let's get back to my first question. How would HGH help a woman who's about to die of cancer?"

He leaned back in his chair, studied me, then shrugged on one side. "My examination didn't lead me to believe Darlene was that close to death. Her last checkup was only six weeks ago. I noted signs of improvement. She'd gained weight, and her color had returned. She also said she'd begun to regain her energy. I require regular monitoring of all HGH patients, since it is a hormone. If anyone fails to comply, I write no more prescriptions. Darlene never missed an appointment."

He'd given me much to think about, but one thing stood out. "You say Darlene wasn't on the brink of death."

"A physician can always make a mistake, but what I saw

leads me to see her death as sudden and unexpected—that is, barring some complication I don't know about. I have no idea what the autopsy discovered."

I sighed. "Liver cancer—"

"Well, well, well," my evil shadow drawled. "What a cozy foursome. I see Wilmont's favorite homegrown snoop has teamed up with the law tonight in a generous serving of Thai and a side of clumsy grilling. Hope you skip the indigestion she usually dishes up with it."

The table wasn't big enough to hide me, so I opted not to crawl under it. A sideways glance caught my tablemates' varied reactions. Dr. Dope looked horrified. I can't blame him. Dutch was brutal and rude. Tedd gaped—I didn't know what to say either. And Chris? Chris's eyes were glued to me, a speculative gleam in those California-surf blues.

It took me a couple of minutes, but I did get my voice back. "I don't see how you can say I'd cause indigestion. You're the one who's disturbed us."

"You're the one poking around their business. I just stopped by for a polite hello."

"Polite? You're out of your gourd. Bella's cats at their worst are more polite than you—"

"Kiddies, kiddies," Lila said. "Why is it that every time I see the two of you, you're locked in a battle of wits?"

The door to the joint was getting quite a workout.

"He's rude—"

"She's a busybody—"

"Hi," she said, her hand extended toward Dr. Dope. "I'm

Lila Tsu, homicide detective with the Wilmont PD. And
you are . . . ?"

The good doctor stood. "I'm Roberto Díaz. From Tijuana,
here on business. Pleased to meet you."

It takes a great deal to surprise Lila, and it takes an experienced observer to catch her well-controlled surprise. The
quick blink and the flare of her nostrils told me everything.
To my satisfaction, she narrowed her eyes.

"Are you Darlene Weikert's Mexican physician?"

Dr. Díaz tightened his lips and gave a curt nod.

The detective's gaze never left his face. "If I might be so
bold . . . what brings you to Seattle?"

"Since I'm certain you'll find out, and since I have nothing to hide, I can tell you I came to settle a loan. Darlene
helped me with the funds I needed to complete the purchase
of a lab that came on the market while I waited for funding
from a European pharmaceutical company."

Lila nodded.

This time I was the one he caught off guard. I hadn't
expected him to tell her about the lab or the funding. He'd
just admitted his need for money. That need cast a shadow
of doubt on his innocence. But then again, would a guilty
man tell a cop that much?

"Well," I said. "It's been lovely, hasn't it, Chris? We
should head on out, don't you think?"

My date gave me an amused look. "I aim to please, Haley.
Let's go."

Dutch snickered.

I glared.

Lila said, "Haley? I hope you remember my previous warnings. Leave the . . . what does Dutch call it? Oh, yes! Leave the snooping to the professionals—us."

I pushed so hard on the table that my chair screeched against the polished cement floor. Every head in the restaurant spun toward me. "Wait'll I get my hands on Tyler Colby!" I muttered. "I can't imagine why he would say we have so much in common. She and I couldn't be more different . . ."

Dutch's outrageous, raucous, and obnoxious guffaws obliterated any effect my mutters might've had on Lila.

One thing's for sure. One of these days that woman, the Wilmont Police Department's pride and joy, will have good reason to jail me. One of these days I'm going to . . . to . . . oh, I don't know what I'll do to that man—those men—but I'm sure it won't be legal.

Question is, which one has it coming first? Tyler or Dutch?

It took hours to get over my snit. It didn't make for a splendid end to my date. I don't blame Chris for his hasty retreat; few men would have known what to do after that disaster.

I punched my feather pillow into a more comfortable blob and pulled my blanket over my shoulders.

Okay. Fine. I let Dutch get to me. Then when Lila followed that up with her warning, I blew up. The best that can be said of my performance is that it provided the patrons of the new Thai restaurant their evening's comic relief. The bad news is that they all watched me act like a toddler in the throes of a tantrum. The good news is that only a handful knew why I stomped out.

Marginally better was that I'd met Dr. Dope. And he was slick, slicker than a five-gallon tub of boiled linseed oil. He was so polished that my gut, which usually reacts in weird and violent ways, refused to consider any feeling about the guy.

Could he have killed Darlene?

Maybe.

He was passionate about his research on and use of HGH. It didn't take too big a hop from there to see him ready to strike out if he felt his work was threatened. Lack of funding always threatens medical research.

On the other hand, I'd now heard twice about the European pharmaceutical firm ready to shell out big bucks for whatever the doc did. Was this for real? Or did he make a habit of knocking off wealthy patients for their money? After all, he didn't need to show any of us where his money had originated.

He also said that in his professional opinion, the Grim Reaper hadn't been hovering around Darlene's bed. Cissy had talked about her friend's upturn in recent weeks. Had both the doctor and the housekeeper lied? Could I believe either one of them?

Or was one, the other, or both blowing smoke on the truth?

I turned on my pillow to check the time on my slime-green-glow digital alarm clock. It was already 2:37 a.m. I wasn't about to come up with any definitive answer in bed. The only outcome I could see to my not-so-good efforts was a massive headache for the next day. One way or another I had to put the Weikert mess out of my mind, if only for a few hours.

I knew only one way to do it. I began to pray.

Of course, morning came too soon for me. But I had snagged a couple of hours' sleep. And I woke up with one thing clear in my mind. I had to check out Dr. Dope, but I couldn't do it the easy way. I couldn't just call Tedd and ask her everything I wanted to know.

It had become much too clear last night that she had some kind of connection to the guy. I didn't know if I could trust anything she said about him. Her observations could be colored by their relationship, whatever it was. Even if she did it in all innocence.

I began to call hotels at eight o'clock. By nine thirty I was afraid he'd registered under an alias and that I'd never track him down. But then I hit pay dirt at the Wilmont Bay Breeze Resort.

Dr. Dope had expensive taste. The Bay Breeze Resort caters to loaded Californians who head north for their Seattle fix. A five-star restaurant takes up half of the main floor of the structure, while the other half is filled with wall-to-wall shopping of the exclusive kind. Original artwork, hand-crafted jewelry, designer clothes, imported cosmetics—the best of the best can be had for a price. Luxury rooms, suites for the most part, fill the second, third, and fourth floors, and a dozen private bungalows dotted the grounds.

I shelled out a hefty price at my local florist shop for a gorgeous bonsai and a card of apology. I figured I had to have an excuse to get close to the doc. My behavior last night merited an "I'm sorry."

While I picked out my miniaturized peace offering, I noticed that the employees at the shop didn't wear uniforms and didn't drive marked cars on deliveries. I knew then I could get away with what I wanted to do.

I hoped.

At the resort, I went straight to the concierge's desk. "Delivery for Dr. Díaz from Paula's Pansy Patch."

"Give me a minute to look him up."

He clicked keys on his keyboard, then looked up. "Yes, he's here. If you'll hand me the plant . . ."

That wasn't the plan. I felt panic spawn. "Ah . . ."

A miracle, Lord. Or at least a lucky break, please!

When the elevator doors opened, I almost laughed with relief. "There he is," I said. "Thanks, but I'll deliver them right now."

With my tree clutched close, I took off at a trot. "Dr. Díaz! Please wait."

He turned, and a frown creased his brow. "Ms. Farrell. I'm surprised to see you here."

"Don't be. I came to apologize for last night. I'm sorry my personal problems ruined your dinner. Here. Enjoy it in good health."

He grabbed the potted plant I shoved at his midriff, then held it out as if it were a new strain of bubonic plague. "You didn't need to go to so much trouble. You didn't ruin my evening."

"Well, I did ask you some pretty direct questions."

"Which I answer all the time. Most people have that same curiosity when they learn what I do. I appreciate the opportunity to talk about my work."

"That's very gracious of you, Dr. Díaz, but there was no need for Dutch's rudeness. And Lila's semi-official warning in a social setting was uncalled for—at least I didn't appreciate her warning me. We certainly soured your dinner."

"No harm done, Ms. Farrell—"

"Last night you agreed to call me Haley. Please do."

"And I'm Roberto."

"All righty, then. Now that we have the unpleasantness behind us, I'll just leave you to continue on your way."

He never voiced the questions I could almost hear grinding inside his head. Instead, he nodded and said good-bye. Because of the tree, he headed back to the bay of elevators. I watched him. While I didn't head out, I didn't follow him either. I just watched the digital display above the elevator until it stopped. Fourth floor.

To this day I can't believe I was ready to pull a breaking-and-entering gig, but I was. And he'd given me at least some of the information I needed to do it. True, I didn't know how many rooms might be on the fourth floor, but I did know one of them housed the doctor. And if I played my cards right, I wouldn't have long to wait until a gossipy house-keeper schlepped down the hall with her cart of sanitizing potions.

When Dr. Díaz crossed the lobby, I ran to the elevator, which whisked me to the right floor in seconds. Since I found the hall deserted, I sat in one of the upholstered armchairs in the landing just beyond the three elevators and pulled out my book. I was ready for a wait.

At 10:49 the rumble of wheels came from the other side of the utility door at the end of the hall. I hurried to open the heavy, leatherette-covered steel slab for the young man who pushed the cart around me.

Oops! I'd hoped for a grandmotherly cleaning lady. Instead, I got a muscle-bound Mr. Clean look-alike. Oh well. Had to play the cards I was dealt . . . or something like that.

To his "Thanks," I replied, "No problem. But I do have a different problem."

He drew his brows together. "'S up?"

Not the most eloquent of males. "I just delivered a plant to Dr. Díaz, and I neglected to give him the packet of special plant food that goes with it." I jiggled the envelope before his nose. "He's gone now, and I don't know his room number. I mean, I can leave it at the desk downstairs, but I'd hate for them to forget. It's a delicate bonsai, and it needs very special care. I'd rather . . . I don't know, maybe tape it to his door."

Mr. Clean Jr. looked at me as though I'd landed from outer space. "Can't he just buy some more plant food?"

"Oh, I'm sure he can. But the bonsai is used to this particular kind. I'm serious. It's a very delicate plant."

Not only had the florist stated that a half a million times, but I'd also heard about the special needs of bonsai plants elsewhere. Not that I had any personal experience with them; I'm blessed with thumbs brown as dirt.

After an excruciating deliberation, he said, "If you say so . . ."

His skepticism crushed my hopes; his jangling keychain revived them.

"Here." He held out his massive left hand. "I'll put the fertilizer in his room."

"It's *not* fertilizer," I said in my haughtiest tone. "It's plant food, specialized bonsai plant food."

"If you say so . . ."

Despite his lack of conversational skills, he checked his computer printout, and then he took the packet of powder and his keys to room 43.

Score! "Thanks."

"No problem."

I left. I knew which room was Dr. Dope's. And with any luck, I'd find a way to jimmy open the door with one of my credit cards. Or maybe my small embroidery scissors would do the trick. I'm not a fan of detailed needlework, but the tiny scissors come in handy when I need to snip off a loose thread in a tight spot. I do work on the occasional redesign and handle antiques for a living when I'm not sniffing out a killer. Or something like that.

I went and did that other work for the next two hours. I didn't make too big a dent in the paperwork at the warehouse, but anything's better than the paper version of the Rockies that had spread across my desk.

Then I returned to the resort—*after* I called and asked for the doctor and was told he wasn't in.

I crossed the lobby as though I belonged there, pushed the fourth button on the wall, and counted the seconds until the elevator stopped. Without any idea how much longer Dr. Dope would be gone, I ran down the hall, credit card in hand, and began to work for real on my life of crime.

It never took off. I had no luck breaking, much less entering.

Plus, I got caught.

"What are you doing to my door?" Dr. Díaz showed me no charm. "No. Don't bother. I'd rather you don't lie. You're working on my lock, and I want to know why you want to invade my privacy."

Since it's said that a good offense is the best defense, I turned, stared him straight in the eye, and hit him with all I had. "Did you kill Darlene Weikert for her money? Were you afraid you'd lose the chance to continue your research without more funds? Did you poison the HGH you sold her? Did you get Cissy to medicate Jacob as well? And have you wormed your way into Cissy's good graces? Is she ready to change her will in your favor?"

Dark, expressive eyes spit rage. "How dare you accuse me of harming a patient? I've always upheld my Hippocratic oath. I'd rather stop my research than hurt someone. If you want a culprit, then take a good look at Cissy Grover. She had the most access to Darlene. If anyone did anything to her, it had to have been Cissy. And now it's time for you to leave. If you don't, you'll force me to call security."

"Your oh-so-self-righteous anger won't protect you if I find even a scrap of evidence against you."

"And your smart mouth won't protect you if I have to call Detective Tsu. Now I understand what last night's fiasco at the restaurant was all about. Just go. Before I'm forced to turn you in."

"Watch your step, Doctor. I'll be watching you."

I walked down the hall, my head high, my back firm, my steps measured and even. I wasn't going to give him the satisfaction of seeing me sweat. Or flee.

By the time I reached my Honda, I knew what I had to do next. It was time to confront Cissy. I had to ask a number of tough questions. And I couldn't let my feelings get in the way. Yes, I liked her, but Jeffrey Dahmer's neighbors had liked him too.

I wasted no time driving to the address Cissy had given me when she told me the Weikert brothers had replaced her with a new nurse. She now lived in the first-floor apartment of an older home that had seen better days. The curtains were drawn, the porch had a dingy wicker chair as its sole embellishment, and most of the paint on the front door had peeled off.

This did not look like the home of a money-grubbing, will-changing swindler.

The short cement walkway wore a generous fringe of scraggly weeds up and down both sides. I made my way toward the front door, and a quiver among the shrubs partway down the right side of the house caught my eye. I craned my neck to see what might have caused the unnatural movement.

Among the leaves I spotted a hint of black. Maybe a neighborhood dog used the overgrown greenery as its preferred and private toilet facility. But then I noticed the broken window above. No dog had done that.

Who'd want to break into Cissy's apartment? It was more than obvious she hadn't lavished funds on this place. I'd be shocked if she had anything of value inside. That left only one other possibility. The broken window had something to do with the Weikert case—there *was* a Weikert case, contrary to popular belief.

The broken window proved it—as if I'd needed further proof.

And then another debacle developed. The hint of black became clearer. That was no dog behind the shrubs. But there was an animal there. Two, as a matter of fact.

First Bali shot out from the bushes. Then Bella fell. Finally, the other cat—maybe *that* was Bali and the first one was the Faux—sped off to parts unknown.

I sighed. "Are you all right, Bella?"

"Nope. My pride's all dinged and danged."

"But otherwise you're okay?"

"I suppose."

"Then suppose some more. Tell me what you're doing here, in the thick of Cissy's wilderness, with your two untamed beasts."

"I'm doing my job, Haley girl."

"I thought your job was the pet detective gig."

"Remember? I have an associate now. To mind the shop."

The hazy picture began to come into focus. "And I bet you gave her a ton of bogus work to keep her busy while you came and busted her window. I have to wonder if this was what lurked behind your supposedly generous job offer."

"The window wasn't my fault," she wailed. "Some know-nothing fool painted the window shut, and when I went to push up the bottom half so I could crawl in, it wouldn't budge. So I pushed and pushed and pushed until my hand slipped."

"Oh no! Did you cut yourself?"

She huffed. "'Course not, Haley. I'm a professional. I wore leather gloves. I don't leave fingerprints, and I do protect my hands."

Bella might be nutty, but she's not dumb. "I'm glad you're okay. But you didn't make it inside the house, did you?"

"Nope. And now who knows where my kitty cats went. Please find them for me."

Yeah, I know. I can't believe I did it either.

On my way down the shabby street, while I called out a series of ridiculous "Here, kitty, kitty, kitties," I tried to figure out how I'd wound up in this ludicrous situation.

But when I lurched forward, arms outstretched, determination at its strongest, and wrestled one of the Balis into a bad excuse for submission, the answer came to me. I groaned. The realization mortified me.

I couldn't avoid the comparison.

Now I knew how I appeared to any observer, herding cats and tangled in their dangling leashes, not to mention how I'd appeared to Dr. Díaz forty-five minutes earlier. Bella had nothing on me. In fact, the comparison put me in the most unfavorable light.

I'd become a younger version of Bella—a nosy busybody, and a clumsy snoop to top it all. Maybe Lila should arrest me, if for no other reason than to protect me from myself.

Goodness knows jail's where Bella needs to be. At the rate she was going, the killer would soon get her.

As soon as he—or she—finished me off.

11

"You owe me big time."

"I'm sorry, Haley girl." Bella's sheepish look screamed how well she knew how much trouble she was in. "How could I know I was going to break a window and slip on rotten leaves, and that the Balis would run away?"

I bit my tongue to stop any snotty comment. A box in my trunk that had once held four gallons of paint served to cage the wildcats in the backseat. Then we got into my car, since Bella had taken her beasts on a walk over to Cissy's.

"Huh? Aren't you going to answer?" Bella is persistent. "How do you figure I'd know ahead of time all this was gonna happen? Huh? Mental telegraphy or something?"

"Gee, I don't know, Bella." I let the blooper go and tried to sit on my sarcasm. "Maybe the window was an out-and-out accident, but anyone who skulks through shrubs has to know what kind of slippery goop lurks beneath." And now covered my passenger seat. "As far as the Balis go? You have to expect the worst when they're around. I've

175

told you a million times. They're a fur-covered threat to the universe."

"Humph! You're just anti-cat."

"I have nothing against cats in general. It's just your two beasts that make me nuts. Look." I held out my bloodied arms. "See what your two 'sweetie cats' did to me? And all I did was try to keep them from becoming urban roadkill."

"Okay, so you did catch Faux before that truck squished her."

"I told you so."

"No need to gloat."

"No need to pretend they're cherubs in fluff either."

"But they only behave like this when you're around. It's your fault."

Yeah, like smog is my fault too. "All right, already. Let's call a truce. Your cats aren't the most innocent around, and I have a rotten time around them. Agree?"

She mulled it over a couple of minutes. "Okay. Truce."

I breathed a sigh of relief. I love Bella. Even though she drives me up and down the wall. Now at least we could talk.

"How about you tell me why you want to break into Cissy's house?"

"Gotta tell you, Haley girl. I really, really like Cissy. And things don't look so great for her right now. With the murder, you understand."

"You've gone out on a kinda lonesome limb with the murder suspicion."

She scoffed. "What about that Larry guy? He thinks his mother got whacked."

"Hey! Watch the language. That's awful." She really had to curb her cable news and Court TV habit. "Okay. So there's the two of you."

"Cissy's sure Darlene got killed, and if you quit being Miss Snooty Pants, you'll admit you think so too. You were the first one, remember?"

I couldn't lie. "Okay. You're right. I do think Darlene was killed. But why would you want to break into Cissy's house?"

"Because I want to find something, anything that'll show us one way or the other how she's involved."

"*If* she's involved." I drew a deep breath. "I know it doesn't look so hot for Cissy, and I like her too. I don't want her to be guilty, but guilt's not something you can cook up after the death. Either she did it or she didn't."

"So how're we going to prove she didn't?"

I stopped for the red light at the corner of Sandy Cove Lane and Whitecap Drive. We were only three blocks away from home, and I didn't know if I could come up with an answer in that short a time. I didn't know if I could come up with an answer no matter how long I took to think.

That's what I told Bella. "But," I added. "There is one thing I can try. I don't know how far I'll get, since I don't have any great connections at the bank, but I'm going to try to check out her finances. There's all that money Darlene 'gave' her. I want to know why, when, how—everything about that gift."

"I can help you with some of that. Cissy had a stump put in one of her arteries."

Stump? "Do you mean stent? One of those jobbies that open up clogged arteries?"

"That's what I told you, Haley girl. A stump. And Cissy needs one of them to try to avoid a heart attack. She's got gunky veins."

Only Bella would translate technical terminology like that. "So she told you she had a pile of medical bills? And that's why Darlene gave her the money?"

"That's what she said. She even showed me her medicines. Not so pretty, so much stuff, you know?"

"I can imagine." So the stent could be verified by following up with a doctor or hospital. "But do you know if she's out of debt now? That apartment looked crummy and cheap."

"What do you want? The Brothers Chromosov kicked her out of the house. She doesn't have much money besides her skimpy Social Security check. That's all she can afford until the estate clears prostate."

I have to pick my battles around Bella. "Karamazov, Bella. The movie's name is *The Brothers Karamazov*."

She shrugged. "You know what I mean. Larry and Tommy are rotten, and they're mean too. Cissy is broke. But I don't want her to be the one who killed Darlene. Even if she needs Darlene's money the most. I'd rather the brothers be the perps. You know, like the ones in the old movie."

I pulled into Bella's driveway. "I already said I like her too, and I don't want her to be guilty, but the person who killed Darlene is guilty, no matter who it is." I jerked a thumb toward the backseat. "Want some help?"

"You want to help me with the Balis?"

"Why not? They already shredded me to pieces. They can't do much worse."

We got the cats into the house with less trouble than I expected. I wound up with only two new gouges and counted myself lucky they weren't all that deep.

"Gotta go," I told Bella. On my way to the door, though, I turned around and on impulse gave her a hug. "I love you in spite of your cats."

Tears filled her eyes. "Love you too, Haley girl. I love you too. So take good care of yourself, and make sure you clean up those scratches. You don't want them to get infracted."

Is it any wonder I always feel dizzy around Bella? At the door I called back, "See ya."

How was I going to get the scoop on Cissy?

I'd have to start at the beginning all over again. With her.

I buckled down for the rest of that afternoon and worked on one of the paperwork peaks. Even though I still had a whole mountain range left to go through after four hours, I felt satisfied with that day's progress.

And I planned my visit to Cissy in the morning.

I brought my secret weapon with me to Cissy's place. Midas was over-the-top thrilled when I uttered that magical, mystical question: "Ride?"

His exuberance piled on the guilt; we weren't going to the park as he expected. But he did ride in the car.

At Cissy's, he spent an eternity sniffing the shrubs. Of course he did. The bushes must've reeked of fresh Balis. Midas is no dummy. He loves to give fresh c-a-t a good run for the money.

When I finally dragged him away, I went up the porch steps, avoided the splintered top board, then made my way to the door and rang the bell. Cissy opened up and immediately slammed the door in my face.

"Hey! Do I have cooties or what?"

"Give me a minute," she called from within. "I have to lock up Garfield. He's not fond of dogs."

Great. I forgot about her love of cats, one of the things she shares with Bella, when I decided to bring Midas. But it was too late to back down. I needed answers, and it was past time for Cissy to give them.

When the door opened again, she was somewhat breathless. "I'm sorry about that. If I'd known you were coming, I'd have made sure Garfield was in the bedroom before you got here. But come on in."

We did, and I sat on the shabby brown and green plaid sofa she pointed to. Midas became a canine vacuum cleaner again, his nose to the ground, sucking up every last hint of new and exciting scent.

"I'm the one who should apologize," I said. "I forgot you were of the Bella persuasion. You're both cat people."

"And you're a dog person. There's nothing wrong with that. They're all perfectly fine animals."

Except the Balis. But why bicker?

Midas's excitement grew by the nanosecond. When he discovered the door that hid the c-a-t, he'd go for it, and then I'd have to drag him away. I had a small window of opportunity here, and I had to climb through it.

"Tell you what. I'm going to cut straight through all the garbage." I didn't want to pretend anymore. "I don't think Darlene died from cancer, but it's not been easy to find anything that'll get the cops to open an investigation. After thinking and thinking until my brain went numb, I realized I had a bunch of questions for you."

"Not more about the HGH, I hope."

"Not really. Those I'm tagging for Dr. Dope."

"HGH is not a drug. Not like you mean."

"Let's just agree to disagree, okay?" When she nodded—not happy about it either—I continued. "My questions for you are about you. About your finances, to make things clear."

"You want to know about the money Darlene insisted on giving me. And she did insist. I wanted a loan to pay off my part of the cost of my procedure—I had a stent inserted—but she wouldn't listen to my arguments. She said her money did no good if it sat in the bank. So she gave me what I needed to cover the bills as they came in."

"So you have no proof that she *gave* you the money."

"No, but I have the bills and the receipts from when I paid them in full."

"That'll help." I was glad she could prove at least that much. Her responses were straightforward, and I hoped she was as honest as she appeared. "So you're all out of debt now?"

"As far as I know, yes. But you know how hospitals operate. Just when you think you're done, they bill you for one more thing they overlooked. I haven't received any new statements in the last seven weeks."

"Would you say you don't need the money Darlene left you?"

She took a moment to consider my question. "I don't *need* the money, but I won't lie and tell you I won't take it." She gestured toward the room's four walls. "This isn't exactly the lap of luxury—not that I'd want that either."

"I understand." And I did. I'd inherited a fortune, and while it provided me with a great deal of material security, I hadn't used the money to change much in my life. "You wouldn't—"

The doorbell cut into my question. I fought down my irritation, but when I saw who'd arrived, that irritation mushroomed.

"I shouldn't be surprised to find you here," Lila said. "But I am. Why are you?"

"Midas and I went for an r-i-d-e, and since I had a couple of questions for Cissy, I decided to stop by."

Midas's wild exuberance went outright ballistic. That's when I noticed that Lila held a leash in her hand. At the end of that leash I found the cutest golden pup I'd seen since Midas was that size.

I managed to get in a question over the *yips* and *yaps*. "That's the little sib, right?"

Lila glanced at her furry companion. "None other."

"Looks just like his older brother did at that age. He's going to be big."

"And just as loud."

I laughed. "Can't deny the truth."

The brothers quieted as they sniffed each other. Then Midas cuffed the little one on the side of the head, and the baby latched onto his floppy ear. The game was on, and in minutes the two went rolling over the floor, their delighted grunts and growls a bizarre background to our equally strange threesome.

"I should leave," I said. "I'm sure you have a reason to stop by, and I doubt it has anything to do with our dogs."

Lila studied Cissy. Then she turned toward me. Finally she shrugged. "If it's acceptable to Mrs. Grover, then I don't care if you stay. It'll save me the effort of telling you later."

I glanced at Cissy and saw the color leach from her cheeks. A buzzard or two swooped in my middle. Lila didn't make visits for no reason at all.

Cissy's voice came out hoarse. "This is about Darlene Weikert, isn't it?"

The detective nodded.

I had to know. "The tox screen results are in?"

She nodded again. "I have to swallow my pride. The tests did turn up something unexpected. Mrs. Weikert had unusually high levels of arsenic in the tested tissues. According to the pathologist, she'd been ingesting the poison for some time."

Although I'd expected it, her confirmation of my suspicion stole my breath away.

Darlene Weikert had been murdered.

I'd thought I'd feel triumphant, but "I told you so" is dull as flat paint when it means a neat lady lost her life through foul play.

"Arsenic?" I asked. "I thought it caused convulsions and that the faces of people who died from arsenic poisoning were fixed in horrible grimaces. Darlene didn't look like that, did she?"

Lila turned to Cissy, then gestured to the empty cushions to my left. "May I?"

Cissy nodded.

"You're right, Haley," the detective said. "That is the normal trademark of arsenic poisoning. But from what the pathologist told me, if a person ingests a steady, increasingly larger amount of arsenic, then the poison doesn't leave its usual fingerprint."

"Arsenic . . ." Cissy leaned forward. "How would Darlene have ingested enough arsenic to kill her, even if in small measured doses? How did the killer get her to take it?"

Lila's eyes narrowed, but her gaze never left our hostess's face. "That's what I'd like to know. You were the housekeeper at the Weikert home, weren't you?"

"I did most of the housekeeping, but I was really there to help with Jacob's and Darlene's medical needs."

"Did you prepare their meals?"

Cissy smiled. "I'm a terrible cook. But Darlene loved everything about it, and she was a genius in the kitchen. She made everything from scratch. Convenience foods insulted her love of good food."

Lila pulled her small notepad from her leather handbag, and with her silver pen, took down a couple of notes. "Did you serve the meals?"

Cissy shook her head. "Darlene loved food. She loved shopping, loved preparing it, and she was very, very particular about the presentation. She always served, even when she didn't feel very well."

I admired Cissy's patience with Lila. I don't know that I could've stayed so calm in the face of the detective's implied accusation.

But before Lila could fire off another question, Cissy spoke. "I'll make your job easier, Detective. I did not put arsenic in the Weikerts' food. Never. I wouldn't have done it under any circumstances, and even less would I have hurt my dearest friend."

Her voice rang with conviction. Even Lila blinked.

"I think," I ventured, "we can assume Cissy didn't sprinkle arsenic on Darlene's spaghetti instead of Parmesan. So we need to find out how it was administered."

Lila's laser gaze speared me. "Why don't you backtrack a couple of sentences, Haley, and get rid of all those *we*s? There is no we here. There's the PD, who will conduct a full investigation into Darlene Weikert's murder, and then there's you. You're the innocent bystander who just happened to suspect murder, because murder is the first thing you think of when someone dies."

"That's not fair, Lila. Even though I did call you right

away, that was a knee-jerk reaction. I don't just paint a mural and stick a killer in it whenever there's a death. Something has to tip me off. The picture of murder was there for anyone to see. Just because you missed it doesn't mean you have to turn snide on me."

"That's not the point," she said. "At least, not right now. We can discuss your odder tendencies at a later time."

I sat back into the lumpy couch. "Go ahead. Grill her some more. I don't know what you're going to get out of her."

Lila shook her head. "I didn't come to grill her. I had questions for Mrs. Grover."

"You girls have problems to solve," Cissy said. "But you can better address them when I'm not around."

"She agrees with me. This isn't the time or place." Lila's satisfaction came as a surprise. Around me she's always so self-assured that I never think she might need approval or support.

Cissy jumped in. "Only when it comes to your argument with Haley."

Lila sighed. "Fine. If you had to take a guess, how would you say the arsenic got into Darlene's system?"

"I can think of only one way." Cissy's expression grew grim. "The HGH. And, yes, I injected her. But I did not mix it with arsenic. I don't know how the poison entered the serum, much less Darlene's body."

"But we agree it was in the HGH," Lila said.

Cissy lifted her chin. "In principal."

"Don't you think," I said, "that if Cissy wanted to kill

Darlene she would have gone about it in a way that didn't point suspicion right at her?"

The gratitude in Cissy's eyes encouraged me. So I added, "I'm not a professional"—I had to appease Lila and her cop pride—"but I think a nurse would know dozens, if not hundreds, of ways to kill someone. She probably also knows how to make it look as if someone else did it."

Lila turned to Cissy. "Is Haley right? Do you know that many ways to kill?"

Cissy stood, anger in her tight lips, her stiff stance, and her blazing eyes. "Any medical professional knows how to kill, just like any law enforcement officer does. That doesn't mean we kill as a matter of fact any more than you do, Detective."

Lila got up too. I had no choice but to follow.

"You understand, Mrs. Grover," the karate chop cop said, "that even though we don't have enough evidence to charge you, we will continue to observe you."

"I know I'm a suspect. But my conscience is clear."

Lila closed her handbag on her notepad and pen. "I hope you have good reason for it." She turned to the peaceful, snoozing dogs. "Come on, Rookie. Let's go home."

Despite the seriousness of the moment, I burst out laughing. "*Rookie?* What kind of name is that for a dog?"

The cop's expression softened as the pup trotted to her. "It just fits."

"You're a dog-owner disgrace. You can't even shake off the cop gig long enough to give your dog a decent name."

She snapped Rookie's leash to his collar, then crossed

her arms, the leash looped around a hand. "And *Midas* is a stroke of genius?"

"Well, it does acknowledge something about the dog himself."

"So does Rookie. He's the new dog in my life. I had a veteran."

Cissy must've had it with the two of us, because she went straight to the door. "You two are so alike that if it weren't for the obvious physical differences, I'd say you were twins. Now please take your sibling rivalry somewhere else."

I glared at the karate chop cop but only called my dog.

Lila didn't respond to Cissy's comment but rather led her pup outside.

When we both stood on the sidewalk, I let out my held breath. "That's ridiculous. I don't know how anyone can say that. You have to be the most inflexible, narrow-minded human I've ever met."

She looked down her small nose—she did even that with panache, so I knew we couldn't have anything in common. "I'd have to say you're the obstinate one. Why you persist in thrusting yourself into situations where you're not welcome or for which you lack even the most basic training is beyond me."

"In a pig's eye! I don't stick myself in. Things happen around me."

She stepped toward her plain-vanilla, unmarked department car. "Do take note of your elegant eloquence."

"Hey! I get my point across." I dragged Midas to my

car. "But remember, if I hadn't 'thrust' myself into the last situation where you definitely didn't want me, then a killer would've gone free."

She stopped. Turned. Nodded. "I can't argue there. You clung to your suspicion, and you pushed and pushed until we did something to prove you either right or wrong."

"See? You can't just dismiss me as a crank. Even you have to admit my instincts were right on."

"I did admit it. What do you want now, an apology to your dented pride, an ode to your suspicious nature, and a bow to your pushier side?"

I let Midas in through the Honda's back door. Then I faced the cop again. "Okay. I get it. I was right, you said so, and now we can get on with our lives."

Rookie chose that moment to whimper. We both turned toward the sweet little guy. "What's wrong?" I asked.

Lila knelt at his side in spite of her chic tan slacks. "Aw . . . baby boy. What's the matter? You want to go home? We did cut into your nap back there. Is that it? Did the brotherly wrestling wear you out?"

The pup nuzzled her hand, then licked away, like every good golden does. Lila reached inside the pocket of her blue blazer. "Here you go. You were a good boy."

And like all good goldens, Rookie nearly took her hand along with the small treat. I laughed. "Oh yeah. He's Midas's brother, all right. Has the appetite to go with the family good looks."

Lila scooped him into her arms, buried her face in his neck, opened her car door, and tucked him inside. Rookie didn't appreciate that kind of treatment. He whimpered again.

"I don't think I've ever thanked you," Lila said. "You were right when you said I needed a dog to keep me sane."

"And this"—I gestured toward Cissy's forlorn house—"was sane?"

She shrugged. "I take my job—"

"Seriously. I know. You've told me that more times than I want to bother to count."

"I do things right, or I don't do them at all."

"I can relate. I don't do things halfway either."

"And that's why you butt heads each time you meet," Tyler Colby said.

We both turned, and for the first time, I noticed the vintage red T-bird parked just beyond our cars. "What are you doing out here?"

As far as I know, Tyler's the only thing Lila and I have in common: our martial arts instructor.

"I'm working with a bunch of guys from my church on a house down here. It's the third one we've renovated for residents who can't afford the work themselves."

Lila tipped her head. "Another of your missionary endeavors, right?"

"I do what I can to follow my Boss." Then he waved his upturned hand back and forth a couple of times. "If I didn't know better, I'd say you two were having a normal, friendly conversation. But I know better, don't I?"

I shrugged. "I can be civil."

"I'm always polite," Lila said.

"But did you notice you two agreed to at least one thing you have in common—that you don't do things halfway? Plus, you're both as pigheaded as they come. Never met anyone more so." He shook his shaved head. "And you say you have nothing in common."

"What movie do you think you're watching?"

"That's so ridiculous, Tyler."

"Give it up, sisters. You could be twins, you're so alike."

I glared.

Lila pursed her lips and narrowed her gaze.

Before either one of us could tell him what we thought of his last statement, he added, "One of these days you're going to be the best of friends. I'd suggest you get used to each other. I doubt it's going to take the Lord much longer to bring that miracle about."

Then he drove off.

The coward.

He couldn't be right . . .

Could he?

12

The next few days were among the most awkward I ever lived through. I focused on work, but that meant I had to spend hours at Tedd's office. While there, I did a great dodge-'em-car impersonation. Every time I bumped into Tedd, I bounced away as far as I could go.

I didn't know what to think of my shrink's date with Dr. Dope, and I suspected the Mexican doc had told her about my bungled attempt to break into his room.

A heart-to-heart with Tedd? Nuh-uh. No way.

But that wasn't my only cause for awkwardness. I still had to work with Dutch. I don't know what troubled me most, the "I get it" moment when I realized it's Dutch who really attracts me, or the sting of his recent spew of nasty comments. Maybe it was a combo of both.

How un-me to let that kind of deal get to me.

Yeah right. After all that's happened to me, I'm a feelings-phobe. And the rumble of emotional crud inside me had me freaking out from one minute to the next, depending on what I saw, heard, or was told.

Not that Tedd or Dutch wanted to have much to do with me.

Even that gave me grief.

Only not so much grief as what headed my way on Thursday afternoon. I'd been at Tedd's office since nine in the morning, marking the hems of the custom-made window treatments. At two fifteen, my cell phone rang.

"Oh, Haley girl," Bella sobbed. "It's so bad . . ."

One thing about Bella: she never cries over nothing. My heart kicked its beat up a notch, and my palms grew sweaty. "What's wrong? Are you hurt? Is it Dad? What do you need me to do?"

She snuffled. "Just hurry. Get to the ER at the Wilmont General Clinic—*fast*."

Father God, give me strength! "Is that where you are? What happened? How'd you get hurt?"

"No, no, no. I'm here, but I'm fine—" Another convulsive sob cut off her words.

Panic shot through me. "What happened to Dad? When did it happen? Where was he?"

"Oh," she wailed. "I'm not doing so good on this. Hale's fine, honey. I'm fine. It's Cissy who isn't."

"Cissy? What's wrong with her?"

"She didn't look so hot when she first came to work, and then a little while ago, she got all sweaty, couldn't breathe worth a dime, and said she felt a cramp all the way down her arm. I figured I'd better call the ambulance, what with her stump and all."

"She had a heart attack." It wasn't a question.

"She sure did. And the doctors are still working on her, so get your fanny over here quick."

I'd already started toward the back door. "Give me five minutes, okay? And don't go freaking out on me. I was doing enough of that for the two of us before you called, so let's not waste twice the energy. Just pray."

"Just hurry."

I snapped my clamshell phone shut, then rapped on Tedd's private office door. When she answered, I turned the knob and stuck my head inside. "I've got an emergency. Don't know if I'll be back today. See ya!"

Even though it was rude, I took off and left Tedd's questions unanswered. There'd be time for answers once I knew Cissy's condition. I hoped and prayed she would survive. I agreed with Bella on this one; Cissy hadn't killed Darlene. I just didn't know who had.

But I was going to find out. For sure.

In my hurry to reach the ER, I sped through a couple of questionable amber lights. I call those hot tangerine. When I pulled into the clinic's parking lot without a cop car's strobe light in my rearview mirror, I allowed myself a sigh of relief.

Bella rushed me, her Brillo Pad hair all aquiver, when I ran inside. "Took you long enough to get here."

"Yeah. All of six minutes, forty-seven seconds. Anything yet?"

"Not a peep, and that scares me. They're still working on her. She must be real bad."

"Not necessarily." I know nothing about emergency cardiac care, but I couldn't let Bella stress out any more. "They may be running tests on her, and you know that can take beaucoup time."

"Don't know about none of those tests, but you're right on the buckets of time."

I had to turn her mind toward something other than what might or might not be happening behind closed doors. "Did anything happen today after Cissy came in to work?"

"Well, she looked super tired, and then she got a call from one of the Brothers Chromosov. She didn't say much, but her face went tomato red. After she hung up, her hands shook like California on a real bad day."

I'd give my Honda to know what Brother Brat had said. "That's the only thing that happened?"

She snorted. "Not hardly. Your detective pal stopped by about forty-five minutes later. I couldn't think of how to hang around and listen in, so it beats me what went on."

"That stress would've done me in. And I don't have Cissy's heart condition."

I heard the *click-click* of high heels. The stride was way too familiar. "Hi, Lila."

"I figured you'd be here," she answered, a wry twist to her mouth. "One of my guys called when he ID'd the patient in the ambulance. Any word on her condition?"

I waved toward Bella. "She knows more than I do."

Lila's smile made me blush. "So you finally admit to someone's superior knowledge. I'm impressed."

"Hey! That's so not fair. I've never said I know more than you or anyone else. But when I'm sure I know something someone else has missed, what do you want from me? To lie about it? To say I don't know when I do?"

She chuckled. "I knew you'd find your way around that."

She faced Bella. "Because she's at least a witness in Darlene Weikert's future murder trial, I'm concerned about Mrs. Grover's trip to the ER. Did anything unusual happen after I spoke with her?"

Bella shook her head, excitement in her eyes. She loves anything that puts her close to the action. "Nothing after you came by, but before's another kettle of clams."

My elderly neighbor has a fine-honed sense of drama. Lila took the bait. "What happened earlier in the day?"

Bella preened. "I got a call, and I recognized the man's voice. It was that sleazy foreign-car-pusher son of Darlene's. He wanted to talk to Cissy."

Lila's notepad and pen put in an appearance. "Did she say anything about the conversation?"

"Nope. Nil. And I tried to ask, all smooth and sneaky-like, you know. But she didn't want to talk about it." She shrugged. "I wouldn't want to talk about that kind of creepy-crawler crud either, so I can't blame her."

"Gee, Bella." I shook my head. "You really dig Tommy Weikert, don't you?"

"I'd like to dig him, all right. Right into solitary coffin-ment." She glanced at Lila. "Do you have any of those dirt pits for his kind here in Wilmont?"

I swallowed a laugh. Lila looked like I feel around Bella: flustered, flummoxed, flabbergasted. Does Bella have a talent, or what?

"Uh . . . no," the elegant cop said. "We don't advocate extreme and cruel measures. We keep solitary *confine*ment prisoners in cell blocks with solid walls and doors, but not in Wilmont. Ours is not that kind of facility."

Bella *hmphed*. "Too bad. Bet that's who whacked the mother."

"Bella, I warned you about that kind of talk."

She tipped up her nose. "They talk like that all the time on that *Real, Regular Cop Arrests* show. If it's good enough for them, then it's good enough for me."

Lila's horror might have been funny if the situation weren't so serious and grim.

In the interest of Bella's preservation, I said, "She's harmless. She just has a thing about bad cop shows, Court TV, and late-night cable news. She needs viewing rehab."

Before Lila could speak, a man in green scrubs pushed through the swinging steel doors to the inner sanctum. "Anyone here for Cecelia Sparks Grover?"

For once Bella, Lila, and I agreed.

"Yes!" we all cried out.

"How is she?" I asked.

Lila held out a card case. "I'm with the Wilmont PD. How soon can I speak with her?"

"I'm her boss and friend." Bella's not the kind to be left out in the cold. "I called the ambulance too."

The confused doctor looked from one of us to the next. He threw up his hands in the universal gesture of surrender. "The patient's in CICU. She's awake, lucid, and asking for Haley and Bella. If you ladies know who they are—"

"Me!" Bella squealed. "Me, me, me! I'm Bella."

The doctor took a long step back.

A tad less wired, I stepped up. "I'm Haley Farrell, sir. Is it possible to see her?"

The leery doctor nodded. "Because she's in intensive care, she's allowed one visitor at a time, and for only ten minutes. I have to ask you ladies for patience. She can see one of you now and another in about an hour."

Lila cleared her throat. "I'm on official business—"

"I didn't think you'd come to play paintball with the patient," the doctor said. "Mrs. Grover is not ready to be questioned."

Lila wasn't happy. I stopped myself from "nana, nana, nana-ing," but only just.

She didn't give up. "How soon can I have about twenty minutes with your patient?"

"Not for a couple of days, and then only if she remains stable, improves even."

I watched Lila from the corner of my eye. She didn't like that answer any better. For a moment she looked ready to argue some more, but then she seemed to reconsider.

She's a smart cookie, all right. That doctor wasn't budging.

Lila was, backpedaling even. "Here's my card. Please call as soon as you're ready to let me do my job."

The guy in green didn't give the card more than a glance. "Inside these walls, Detective Tsu, you only do your job after I've done mine."

He spun and marched back to the swinging doors. Before he shoved his way through, he stopped. "Haley can see

Mrs. Grover first, then next hour Bella gets a chance. The detective can wait for my call."

I chuckled. "Don't hold your breath, Lila. He's not smitten with you. Let's see if you take it as well as you dish it out."

Lila shrugged. "I'll see Mrs. Grover, just not today."

"Can I buy a seat for the battle royal?"

"There won't be a battle, Haley. I'm a professional."

"And if you go into your 'I'm so serious about my job I do so well' bit, I'll scream."

Now she smiled. "Please do. I'd love to see security drag you away."

I licked my index finger and chalked one up for me. "You won't see that, but you will see me tread where cop woman has yet to go. One small step for Haley, one giant step for . . . for . . . Oh, I don't know. You get my drift."

She shook her head on her way out of the waiting lounge. Hey, I felt pretty good. This was the first time I'd gotten the better end of the stick around her.

"You're staying here?" I asked Bella.

"What d'you think, girlfriend? I'm going nowhere until I see Cissy. So get a move on already. The sooner you see her, the sooner I get to go in."

Even though I wanted to see Cissy, when I walked through the swinging doors, bad memories did a number on me. Not only had I spent two hideous days in ICU after I was raped, beaten, and left for dead, but I also put in hours there during my mother's last days.

I wanted out as much as I wanted in.

With every step my gut twisted tighter. The mediciney

stink did weird things to my brain, and that wacky brain
of mine in turn detonated my "Go. Split. Run, outta here,
fly!" alarm. But I wanted—no, needed—to see Cissy. She'd
asked for me. I had to know what she wanted.

At the nurses' station, I got directions to Cissy's room.
Although the curtains around the bed had been swapped
from green to blue-gray, the room looked just like the ones
my mother and I had stayed in. It had the same glass walls
so staff could keep the patient in sight at all times, and once
I stepped inside, the same eye-popping spread of electronic
monitors, gauges, tubes, valves, and who knows what else
made my stomach flip. Queasy pangs hit when I rounded
the column of privacy curtain at the foot of Cissy's bed.

Cissy was small, and the bed with its steel bars, the IV
stand at her left, the oxygen tube at her nose, and the monitors behind her dwarfed her slight form beneath the white
sheets.

"Hey," I said in a loud whisper. "I hear you asked for
trouble. They sent me."

A weak smile did little to brighten her face. "You're not
half bad."

"How are you?"

The smile gave a wobble before it drooped. "I'd like to
get my hands on the elephant who thought my chest made
a comfy seat."

"Do you still have a lot of pain?"

"Not really. They pumped me full of all kinds of meds,
and I'm more comfortable now. But that's not why I asked
for you."

As she spoke she tensed up. The wiggles on one of the monitors staggered out of their regular pattern.

"Stop that!" I tried to sound stern. "Don't stress out. It won't help you get well. Besides, I'm on the job now. I'll do all the stressing for both of us."

Her smile returned, and even though I almost needed a microscope to see her shoulders ease a tiny bit, I did see it happen.

"You're about as bossy as Bella," she said. "But give you forty-some more years, and you'll be just like her."

"I don't think I like that prognosis. I'll have to give it some thought—later. Now why don't you tell me why you wanted to see me?"

She sighed. "You know how things look for me in Darlene's death. But I also think you realize that I couldn't have done such a thing. I'm afraid Detective Tsu doesn't agree. She's ready to arrest me. But, Haley"—she grabbed my wrist—"I didn't do it. And I'm so scared I'll die in jail."

Her cold fingers shook in spite of her tight grip. I had to reassure her.

"Now listen to me. I'm going out on a limb here, but I promise you won't die in a jail. You won't even spend a minute in a cell—not if I can help it. And I'm sure I can."

The fear in her eyes reached out and struck me.

I barreled on. "But there's one thing you have to do. And that's ditch the fear. It's more toxic than the arsenic that got Darlene."

She refused to look me in the eye. "It's easy to say but much harder to do."

"It is when you go it alone."

"I'm not alone anymore," she said. "I now have you and Bella."

"But we're not the ones who can help you, not with this. There's only one person who can do that, and that's God through his Son. God stretches his hand out to you, Cissy. All you have to do is take it and believe."

"You make it sound so easy."

"It's the easiest thing you'll do in life. What can be better than to lean on the King of Kings, the Maker of everything? They don't say he has the whole world in his hand for nothing."

Her fear made me want to cry.

"I don't think I could stand it if I put my trust in God and then he just wasn't there after all."

"Won't happen. Give him a chance. He'll draw you closer all the time. Come on. Just say, 'Yes, Lord. I've been a mess on my own, but I'm yours now.'"

"That sounds simpler than what I've heard."

"That's all God asks for. He wants us to admit we're sinners ready to live his way."

Cissy closed her eyes. For a moment I thought she'd fallen asleep—she had said she was full of meds. But then her lips moved.

"Yes, Lord. I've been a mess on my own, but I'm yours now."

Thank you, Jesus.

I took her hand. I also took the prayer reins—so to speak.

I thanked the Father for his love, I praised him for all his mercies, I asked his forgiveness for any and all sins, I prayed for his strength during Cissy's illness, and I asked for wisdom as I tried to help her.

Cissy's soft amen felt like yet another of God's blessings, and he's been very generous, in many ways. His Word too never fails to comfort me.

Which reminded me . . . "Do you have a Bible?"

"Last one I had was the one my mother gave me back . . . You know? I think I was still in junior high."

I opened the top drawer of the nightstand by her bed. "Here. Just as I remembered. There was one in my mother's room too."

"It won't do me much good if I can't read it. I've had a hard time since I left my reading glasses at the Weikerts' when you and I visited Jacob. I haven't had time or money to buy new ones."

"I may not be as hairy as Midas, but I do a pretty mean fetch," I told her. "He's trained me to the max."

"Our pets own us more than the other way around," Cissy said with a smile. "And I'm going to have to ask another favor—"

"Say no more. Super Haley to Garfield's rescue."

A nurse stuck her head around the edge of the curtain. "I'm sorry, but you've stayed longer than the legal ten."

I winked at Cissy. "Busted! Bada-bing, bada-bang! Gotta move, gotta groove. Now behave, you wild woman, you. I'm sure Jacob's new nurse will help me look. I'll be back with those glasses in no time—if Sarge here lets me in again."

The redhead in funky bedpan-bedecked scrubs grinned. "Every hour on the hour, ten minutes at a time. And who knows? You might be good medicine for Mrs. Grover, so I'll let you in—as long as you play by my rules."

I tapped my forehead in a crummy imitation of a military salute. "You got it." With another smile for Cissy, I headed out. "I'll be back later, okay?"

Her soft "okay" followed me all the way to the Weikerts' home.

Dave, Jacob's new nurse, answered the door on my first ring.

"Good to see you," he said. "I figured you'd be back sooner or later."

Guilt gnawed at me. "I'm sorry, but I can't stay long this time, not long enough for checkers. Cecelia had a heart attack. She's at the clinic, in ICU. She asked me to stop by to see if you would help me find the glasses she left behind."

"Is that who they belong to? I tried them on Jacob, but you can imagine the frame didn't fit. And Tommy and Larry insist they weren't their mother's either."

"Now you know."

"Let me get them for you."

The husky man hurried down the hall, and I took a good look around. The house had awesome potential. Its good bones lent the surface shabbiness a certain dignity.

I took a peek at the dining room, a vast space across the foyer from the parlor. Gorgeous mahogany built-ins needed nothing more than a good cleaning and maybe a light coat of shellac—I prefer the older, more natural finishes when old wood is in decent condition. The striped gray-green wallpaper and faded ivy-print wall-to-wall carpet? Those had to go.

Once Cissy recovered and the estate cleared probate, I hoped I could talk her into letting me bring this grand old dame back to where she should be.

"Who're you?"

Jacob stood at the top of the stairs, confusion on his face.

"It's Haley, Jacob. We've met a couple of times. Remember? We played checkers with Cissy the other day."

The man had a great smile. "Checkers?"

"Yes, but I can't stay today. Cissy's sick, and she needs me to take her reading glasses to her. She left them here when we played checkers."

"Glasses? I think I'm thirsty."

Dave joined me. "Cecelia's glasses." Then he looked up at his charge. "You want to come down, Jacob? I've got iced lemonade in the kitchen."

I whispered, "I'll be on my way."

Dave nodded. "Sorry. I can't let him go to the kitchen on his own."

"I understand. I'll bring Cecelia back as soon as she's out of the hospital."

"We'll be here."

When I left, the door closed with a soft click. I hurried down the steps, my thoughts on the sadness I'd seen today. The only spark of light was Cissy's willingness to trust God, even if it had taken a close brush with death to bring it about.

Nothing would bring light to Jacob's shadows again.

Alzheimer's is a relentless thief, and it had him in its clutches.

When I reached the sidewalk, a woman called out. "You! You there. Can you tell me how Jacob is these days? I'm Audrey Crombie, by the way. I've lived here for forty years."

The senior citizen next door held an activated high-pressure hose in her right hand. It had the look of a semi-lethal weapon.

"So how is he?" she prodded.

"What can I tell you? He's in the fog that comes with dementia. The last time I saw him, he played checkers, but he only moved the pieces when and where Cissy said. Today he seems as confused as can be."

She tsk-tsked. "Darlene and Cissy did everything they could for him. He's had the best doctors, even took him to that fancy psychologist. She seemed to help a little. Although I don't know if what Darlene called improvement was more how she saw things after her counseling sessions."

"That sounds like Tedd's touch, all right."

"Oh, you know their psychologist?"

Way more than I wanted to say. "I'm an interior designer. I'm redoing her office right now."

"She really takes her job to heart, you know. She'd stop by from time to time. She even visited the afternoon Darlene died."

"Really? I was here that day, and I didn't see her." Neither had Tedd mentioned that visit to me. Interesting.

The hose turned, and I caught a splash of spray. "Sure. She was here. She and that foreign doctor Darlene thought so much of. They came by . . . oh, somewhere around two thirty, no later than three."

Hmm . . . Tedd and Dr. Dope. Together again. At the scene of the crime. Tedd had questions to answer.

"Well, Mrs. Crombie, it's been nice to meet you, but I have to hurry. Cissy suffered a heart attack earlier today, and when the doctor let me in to see her, she asked me to get her reading glasses. She left them here the last time she played checkers with Jacob."

I waved the half-moons.

She smiled. "That Jacob and his checkers. Tell Cissy I'm so sorry to hear, that I wish her the best recovery. Let her know I'll stop to see her sometime next week."

"No problem. And I'm sure she'd love a visit."

In my car, I took a moment to consider what I'd just learned. I tried to connect A to B to C but had no luck. My temper, on the other hand, tied itself in a too-tight knot, and I began to fume.

Why hadn't Tedd mentioned her visit—with Dr. Dope, no less?

I turned the key in the ignition. *Okay, Lord. I can stew here from now until the rapture, but that won't get me anywhere. I have to see Tedd to ask my questions, and I'm scared stupid to hear what she might say.*

The car purred to life and rolled into traffic, and I worked to evict my thoughts. But I failed.

Father, help me. I don't want to make things worse by blurting something dumb—and you know how good I am at it.

I pulled up to the strip that houses Tedd's office. With a

soul-deep sigh and a mind-boggling amount of reluctance, I locked my car and went inside. I made myself ignore the two clients in the waiting room and glared when Willa tried to stop me.

"It's an emergency," I said.

"But—"

"Trust me. I'll handle it."

Her look said she wouldn't trust me with yesterday's rolled-up newspaper, much less her job, but I was fresh out of patience. Something stunk here, and I refused to take another no, any more dips and dodges, or stumbling blocks of any kind for an answer.

The oh-so-discreet shrink had gone to her private office, since she'd just finished with one client and had yet to meet with the next. I barged on in.

"Okay, Tedd. Spill the beans. What's up with you and Dr. Dope? And why didn't you tell me you both went to Darlene's house right around the time the coroner says she breathed her last?"

A blush darkened Tedd's smooth caramel complexion. "I'm at work, Haley. I have two clients to see before I'm done. Why don't you meet me at Mickey D's at around eight?"

"Because my questions are easy ones. We don't have to eat crummy fast food to hash them out. Just give it to me straight, and I'll get out of your hair."

Something flashed in her eyes. If I didn't know her so well, I would've called it fear. But the Tedd I know is fearless; she's gone through the worst and is now a stronger woman.

She stood and rolled her chair out of her way. She rounded

the desk and met me toe-to-toe. "You know why I didn't say a word. Your suspicious mind would have convicted Roberto in a blink. Maybe even me, and I didn't have a thing to do with Darlene's death. Neither did he."

Once she said it I knew why she'd failed to talk. But what I also knew was that she'd danced around the most important question.

"Don't mess with me, Tedd. What's the deal with Dr. Dope? Why do you want to protect the guy? He's one of the most likely suspects. He had motive, opportunity, and means. You know what I'm saying?"

The tilt of her head, the tight clasp of her hands, the quick flutter of her eyelids all squealed on her.

My earlier queasiness returned, and with a vengeance.

I knew then. Even before she spoke.

But she did speak after a minute or two. "Remember the relationship that almost made it to the altar? I came within four months of becoming Mrs. Roberto Díaz. I broke it off the week before Darlene died."

I almost didn't make it to the ladies' room. This time, though, I didn't throw up. I just stood over the toilet and gagged.

Tedd and Dr. Dope. Is it any wonder the idea made me sick?

13

No matter how I slice it, the next few minutes were the worst I've spent around Tedd. She has now witnessed my twitchy stomach's betrayal a couple of times. The first time, my past caught up with me. The other, my doubts about Dutch's innocence did me in. I didn't want to learn he'd committed a crime just when I'd begun to feel the attraction.

Pretty scary stuff.

But this? This was the worst of the worse. Tedd's my shrink, for goodness' sake! She's my friend, even. In many of the ways that count, she knows me better than anyone else—even me. I've trusted her with my darkest secrets, my worst fears, my secret thoughts, dreams, and hopes. Just to think she might be involved in Darlene's murder pushed me beyond what I could . . . well, stomach.

But I didn't throw up this time like I did over Dutch. I should see that as progress.

Whoopee.

Tedd came after me. "Haley? Are you all right?"

I couldn't question her sincerity; she cares for me. But still . . .

"Just peachy dandy. No big deal, you know? I find out every day about a friend's romance with a guy who peddles voodoo meds to desperate people. Oh! And the guy's always suspected in the murder of one of his desperate buyers."

"Come on, Haley," she said from the other side of the white stall door. "That's ridiculous, even for you. Roberto has researched HGH for years, and he didn't do a thing to Darlene. You know it."

"I don't know it from snickerdoodles. Arsenic killed Darlene, and the HGH looks like the carrier pigeon for the poison."

"That doesn't mean Roberto poisoned the serum."

"Who sold it to her? He even bought the lab that makes it."

"Cissy, who's still alive and kicking, took it too."

"Just barely."

"What does that mean? Just barely what?"

"She's the emergency that dragged me away earlier today. Cissy had a heart attack. She's in the ICU at the clinic."

"I suppose you blame Roberto—maybe me—for the heart attack."

"No, but I might if there's reason to suspect foul play."

She sighed in frustration—I've learned to interpret her sighs. "I should expect you to say that kind of thing."

I hadn't gagged since she walked in, so I opened the door. "How come?"

She crossed her arms and tapped the toe of her leather pump on the floor. "You're obsessed with murder. You'd suspect foul play even if the FBI, CIA, and NSA had the deceased under surveillance at all times."

"Sure. Why not? Who's to say a spook didn't snuff the poor schmuck because the surveillance detail got to him?"

"I quit. I've had all I can take. Roberto didn't kill Darlene, and neither did I. Now, if you don't mind, I have clients who need my help. You're way beyond me." Her shoulders drooped. "And here I thought you knew me. You have to do something about your trust issues, you know."

"Hey, I took up scuba diving like you wanted—"

Tedd closed the bathroom door on my defense. It's just as well. I'd probably have babbled something stupid, something I would regret sooner rather than later. And she's right. Scuba diving aside, I don't do trust.

The cold-water splash at the sink felt good on my face. I wished I could wash away all the crud crammed inside my head. Then maybe I'd have a chance to sift through the leftovers and come up with answers. But life doesn't work that way.

I did need help. *Father, help me, please. I hope there's nothing there . . . that Tedd's as innocent as she says. And please, please? Don't let her hate me.*

Since I'd worked right through lunch, my backbone decided to tickle my belly button. Maybe food would put a damper on my stomach's acrobatics. The deli next door makes a mean chicken salad sandwich, and today it hit the spot. Once done, I trudged back to Tedd's office, super-sized latte in hand.

I returned to the meeting room, where I'd been when Bella's call about Cissy came through. Since then a large crate with my name on it had arrived. No missing fancy-schmancy Guatemalan leather chairs there, of course, but I did find the Mexican blankets I'd slated for throw pillow covers for the waiting room and new upholstery for the meeting room chairs. Since I think better when my hands are busy, I stacked the blankets by color, chose the ones with a future as pillows, and then draped the others over the chairs.

I love it when a plan comes together.

With little more than a twist or two of my Phillips-head screwdriver, the cushions came off the chair frames. I spread the blankets on the floor, scoped out the best chunks to use, measured, and cut. My trusty pneumatic staple gun had taken up residence at Tedd's the day I started the redesign, and thus armed, I attacked the chairs.

Six of twelve chairs later, Tedd came by. "I'm done for the day. You can stay as long as you need. Use the back door to leave, and make sure it locks behind you. Oh, I'm setting the alarm, since you're here alone."

I couldn't make myself look at her, so I murmured a vague "mm-hmm."

The thunk of the outside door bounced off the walls. I slumped against the nearest of those walls and slid to the floor, my muscles unable to hold me now that the adrenaline rush had passed.

Tedd's defense still rang in my head. Was she right? Or had she maybe protested too much?

I tried to pick my way through the avalanche of thoughts. Then the back door opened again, but no alarm blared.

"Did you forget something, Tedd?" I asked.

Instead, Dutch walked in. "No. I let myself in because I need measurements to custom build floor-to-ceiling bookcases for that back wall. I don't want to mess up the order when I call the lumberyard tomorrow."

A giddy cobbler found a home in my head; his little hammer pounded out a steady beat. I rubbed my forehead. What else would go wrong today?

"Don't let me keep you from your work," I said.

"Are you okay?"

"I'm fine."

Sure, I was. That's why my voice broke and tears formed. It took a genius to figure it out. Not.

No genius, but no dummy either, Dutch came over and joined me on the floor. "What's up?"

His voice swirled like silk around me, and his eyes showed only concern. My tears did their thing. Hot and copious, they flooded my cheeks, pooled in the corners of my lips, dropped off my chin. I've never been the kind to cry in dainty sobs and delicate droplets. Nope. I'm the kind with the Rudolph schnozz, bunny-rabbit red eyes, fire-engine cheeks kind of tears.

Okay, so I bawled.

Dutch reached over and took my hand. "Don't know

what's up, but it's probably good for you to cry it out. I'll wait. I don't have anywhere else to go."

My sobs broke too hard for me to spit a zinger at him. I don't know if I would have even if I had been able to. I clung to his hand and cried some more.

When I didn't have one more tear left in me, I swiped my sopped cheeks with the back of my free hand. My breath came in shuddery gusts, my throat hurt, my eyes stung, my nose burned.

Dutch gave my fingers a soft squeeze. "Wanna talk?"

"I owe you an explanation."

"You don't owe me a thing. I'm just glad I was here. Misery is the pits, and it's worse to sit and cry all alone."

I arched a brow. "*You* know my kind of misery?"

"I've been around more than thirty years. Not all of them have been so hot."

"That lawsuit over the house that slid down the hill."

"Among other things."

"Must feel good to be cleared of that stain."

"Trust me, you wouldn't have a clue."

I gave a raw chuckle. "Maybe not about lawsuits, but I've had more than my share of pain."

"Looks like you're having more right now."

"You could say that." I drew in another deep breath and came to a decision. "Please don't give me grief about my curiosity, okay? This isn't the time for a joke or one of your snide jabs."

He reached over, placed a finger under my chin, and turned my face to his. "Torture's not my thing, Haley. You're down right now, and I've never lashed out at someone who's down. I may kid around, but I don't hurt people."

Why I decided to trust him, I'll never know. "It's about Tedd. She was at the Weikerts' with the sleazoid doc the afternoon Darlene died. Would you believe it?"

"Interesting . . . but I don't think I'd call Dr. Díaz a sleaze. Unorthodox maybe, but not shifty or crooked."

"Even if it looks like someone poisoned Darlene's HGH? He's the one who sold her the serum, and he's bought the lab where it's made—with a loan from Darlene, no less."

"And you can convict the guy on that?"

"I haven't convicted him. But he doesn't answer questions, and I bump into him everywhere I turn."

"He has legitimate business in Seattle."

"He could have the illegitimate kind too."

"Hypothetically, that's true."

"He was at Darlene's house the day she died. I have to wonder if he didn't give her a little extra nudge to hurry the end even more."

"Someone gave her something that day. She was poisoned."

"Not in the usual way. She took in the arsenic over a period of time. At least, that's what the pathologist who ran her toxicology screen told Lila."

"And she told you? My, my. Aren't we chummy these days?"

"She didn't share privileged info, if that's what you mean. Cissy asked for the extra tests on Darlene's body, and Lila stopped by to give her the results when I was there."

"For tea and crumpets, I presume."

I blushed. "I had questions for Cissy."

He chuckled. "I figured as much."

"You promised you wouldn't make fun of me."

"Okay, okay. You're right, I did." He drew his brows together. "Didn't you say you were upset over Tedd? How do you connect the dots here? Other than she counseled Darlene."

"I told you. She was at the house that day with Dr. Dope."

"You don't mess around, do you? What a thing to call the guy."

"I could call him Killer, but you'd like that less."

"Can you blame me? You're not just jumping to conclusions, you're taking flights of fuzzy faith and crash-landing on mounds of quicksand."

"Okay. I could be wrong. But things don't look so good for the doctor right now. And Tedd's in the thick of it."

"Because she knows the guy? Because of her visit?"

"She doesn't just know the guy, Dutch. She nearly married him. And she rivals the NFL's best defensive end when it comes to the doc."

He let out a low whistle. "She dated Dr. Díaz? Then you have to take whatever she says with a mountain of salt."

"Now you're getting it. And there's more: she never said a thing about their romance. She didn't even tell me she knew the guy."

"Why would she share her personal life?"

"Because she's my friend."

"You sure about that?"

"I'm not sure about anything anymore. But I thought better of her. I trusted her."

"And you don't trust me—even after I saved your hide a couple of times."

"It's different. Tedd's my shrink."

He waggled his eyebrows. "So you do need a shrink. For real."

"Don't laugh. That's serious. Only that little tale's not for tonight." I reached out and grabbed his hand. "Don't you get it? I can't stand to think she might have had something to do with Darlene's death."

He laced his fingers through mine. "That's rough. I don't blame you for being upset. Remember though. Tedd would need a pretty good reason to want Darlene dead. Does she?"

"That's just it. I don't know how far she'd go to protect Dr. Dope. His research is like his whole life."

"She must have been a big part of that life at some time."

"Not so long ago either. She says she broke up with him the week before Darlene died."

"I hear your skepticism—again. Why?"

"Didn't you see them at the Thai restaurant the other night? They were together. What if she lied and didn't break up with him after all?"

"Why would she lie?"

"She might want to stay out of the cops' radar."

"It didn't help her dodge yours."

"But why wouldn't she tell me about her engagement? Why didn't she talk about the upcoming wedding? Why wouldn't she say a thing about the breakup? Why wouldn't she trust me?"

"Maybe it's not about trust. Maybe it's about the kind of person she is. You know, the private kind."

"But she didn't say a thing, not even when I told her about you—"

I bit down on my tongue. I couldn't believe I'd said that, what I'd almost confessed to him.

Get a grip, Haley.

He narrowed his gaze but didn't mention my slip. "So if not Tedd or Cissy, and if we put the doctor aside for a while, who do you think killed Darlene?"

I was still shaken by my slip. "Ah . . . well . . . um, maybe the sons. They have lots of dollar-sign motives. Neither one's your usual bean counter, lawyer, trash collector, builder, or cook."

"Aren't they both independent?"

I hooted. "Darlene still had to spring for Tommy's clothes, for goodness' sake. And that's after she forked over his trust fund a few years ago."

"What about his car dealership?"

"Darlene footed that bill too."

"Hmm . . ."

"Yeah, pal. Hmm to the max. And the day you saw me there, he got a call from someone who put the squeeze on him for money. It sounded like he'd been sure he'd inherit Darlene's dough with Larry, had gone out and rung up a whopper tab somewhere but then had to face the music with his usual empty pockets."

"Now I see where you're going with this."

"That's not all. Larry's another piece of work. He's the ultimate techno-nerd with a thing for the newest, spiffiest hardware that comes down the pike. He blew his trust fund on electronics of the outrageous-price kind."

"But if that's the case, then he should be set. Techo-nerds are the modern-day silver barons. Why would he kill his mother?"

"Shows how much you know. Cissy told me he feels the equipment's obsolete the minute he hauls it out of the store. He's always 'investing' in that stuff, and he'd hit up Darlene every time he got the itch to upgrade."

Dutch whistled. "Electronics don't come cheap. There is a reason for his wired state, isn't there? I mean, he does use it in a business, doesn't he? Or are you saying he sponged off Darlene too?"

"No one's sure what he does. He does have a home. The deed's in his name. I checked—that's easy to do."

"Maybe Darlene bought that too."

"Sure. Why not? But if both mooched off her so much, would they really want her gone? She never seems to have said no."

"Maybe she finally did. They must have been desperate. Maybe they gambled for the whole inheritance . . . and then lost."

"That's why I have to check out their finances. And I have

to look into Dr. Dope's—sorry, Dr. Díaz's—business. We only
know that Tommy's a mess and Larry's just strange."

"Never thought I'd see the day, but you know? I think
you're right. We have to nose around these guys' businesses."

A shimmer of hope made me smile. "So you're with
me?"

He squeezed my hand. "You do make a funky kind of
sense."

I shot him a glare. "Watch it, buster!" Then I faced the
single largest obstacle. "Have any brainstorms on how to
do it? I'm fresh out of snooping ideas."

"Actually, I do. You remember Ron Richardson?"

"How can you even ask? It's not as if I stumble over
people's dead daughters every day."

"He's got more connections than the California power
grid."

"I hope his don't black out as much as California's do."

"Let's give him a chance, okay?"

"Count me in."

We made plans to meet with Ron as soon as the busy
man could spare the time. Then Dutch stood and gave me
a hand up, but he didn't release my hand. When I gave him
a curious look, I had to catch my breath.

His eyes glowed with . . . tenderness? I wasn't sure, but
whatever it was, it touched me somewhere deep inside.
His mouth curved in a gentle smile unlike any I'd ever
seen on him.

And then he really did it. He pulled me closer, wrapped

his arms around me, and cradled my head against his chest. What totally blew me away was my response. Instead of backing up, all my danger alerts firing, panic multiplying like termites in damp wood, I shocked myself and leaned into his warmth.

We stood there for long minutes. I welcomed the strength of his arms. I felt the rise and fall of his breath. I heard the steady beat of his heart.

"You're something else, you know?" Dutch whispered.

"How? Like a mold and mildew plague?"

He gave me a squeeze. "No, more like a daring two-year-old."

I pulled away as far as his iron-bar arms let me go. "That's not nice, Merrill. I don't do tantrums."

Usually.

"It's not about tantrums. You're innocent and bold, and it just gets me."

"So I'm naive and reckless?"

This time he treated me to a gentle shake. "Quit twisting my words, will ya? Let me pay you a compliment. You step out with a brand of courage most people can't imagine. I get the feeling you'll do whatever it takes to see justice done."

"Chalk one up for the smart cookie! I could never stand to see a rotten slug get away with murder or theft or . . . whatever."

"Yep. You're a one-woman crusade, all right."

"I wouldn't go that far, but if there's something I can do, I have a responsibility to do it."

"I don't get that responsibility thing, but you wear your

gutsy spirit on your sleeve. Sometimes I think you don't know fear and have no clue what self-preservation means. I can't decide whether to buy you a leash for your own sake or beg you to let me in on your secret for bravery."

I shuddered. "Trust me, Dutch. I know fear better than most. I faced the worst humanity can dish out and, by the grace of God, lived. I do have a healthy sense of self-preservation. It's just that I've come to realize I'm not in control. The best decision I ever made was to turn everything over to God."

"So you use faith as a reason to indulge your snoopier side."

That topic would keep for another time, so I jabbed a finger into his hard chest. "Face it, Builder Boy. You're just jealous. I've been right way more times than you."

"Let's see how right you are this time."

"Set up a date with Ron, and I'll sniff out our perp."

He chuckled. "Ron was pretty impressed with you. Let's see how he feels about your dog-with-a-juicy-bone ways when he's on the receiving end of your need to know."

"I'm not going after him, so he'll be fine. I only want him to help me figure out what's the deal with all these people."

You could've knocked me over with a feather at his next stunt. With a smile as wide as Puget Sound, Dutch leaned down and pressed a kiss onto my forehead. Then he let go, tapped the tip of my nose with a finger, and added, "Come on. I'm going to follow you home—to make sure you stay out of trouble."

I went into warp drive: packed up, locked the office, flipped the alarm back on, hurried to my car, turned the key, threw it in gear, and drove home with the radio blaring into the night. I didn't want to think about what had just happened.

I exhaled my relief when I parked in my driveway. But Dutch again shocked the socks off me. He parked on the street and ran to the driver-side door.

"What's the deal?" I asked, my voice less shaky than I felt. "Don't you have a home?"

He shrugged. "It's a lonely place."

I got out of the car and shot him a grin. "Get a dog."

"Like you told Lila, huh?"

"Guilty as charged." I went to the porch, my six-foot-plus shadow still attached. "And it worked. Rookie's urgent toilet needs have put a dent in her cop shop obsession."

He laughed loud and hard. "I can't see the cover-model cop doing the poop-scoop thing."

"That was Dr. Farrell's exact prescription for her. Picking up your pet's doggy doo puts life into perspective."

When I opened the door, the sounds of Armageddon sucker punched me. Bella and Dad were going at it pretty good.

Dutch laid a hand on my shoulder. "What's up?"

"Beats me. They rarely see eye to eye, but they don't usually fight. It sure sounds like they need a referee this time. Let's go."

We marched into the kitchen, from whence the verbal cannon fire sallied forth.

"How could you?" Bella bellowed.

"I forgot." Dad's voice rang louder than I remember ever hearing it. "It just slipped my mind."

"That's the thing, Hale. It's not as if church board meetings pop up in the pumpkin patch. They happen every month. What'd you do instead?"

He frowned, rubbed his forehead, then shrugged. "I don't think I did much of anything. How did you know I missed the meeting?"

Bella mimicked a phone to the ear. "Hello, Hale. It's me, Bella Cahill. I'm the one who writes your church newspaper. Every month. Have for four years. No one's ever told me I'm that easy to forget. Who d'you think puts the meeting schedule in that very same newspaper?"

"Well, sure, but—"

"No buts, then. I know when the meetings are supposed to happen, and I know when I see your bedroom light from across the street right around when you're supposed to be Robber Ruling at the church that you missed the dumb meeting. Did you forget my new career? Did you forget who I am? Huh?"

I sputtered, then laughed.

"You, Bella?" Dad asked. "I couldn't forget you no matter how hard I tried. *If* I tried."

She preened. "Aw, Hale. How sweet."

Dad gave a totally un-Dad snort. "You might be nutty, unpredictable, sassy, and a brazen imp, but the one thing you're not is plain old sweet."

Outrageous. I'd never heard Dad and Bella do this.

She whooped. "You sure know how to flatter a girl, you silver-tongued charmer you. How did your late wife put up with you all those years? Especially if that's the kind of sweet nothings you whispered to her."

"Different woman, different personality."

Enough of the weirdness. "Hey! Time-out, guys. Dad, call the board members. Tell them you forgot, that aliens sucked your brain out, whatever. Bella, back in your corner. Better yet, go check on your beasts. Both of you, take a break, rest up, prepare your ammunition for the next fight."

"We weren't fighting." Bella stuck her pugnacious chin out to the max. "Hale messed up, and I had to tell him."

Dad snorted—again!

I glared. "It doesn't matter if you call it break dancing to wails and howls courtesy of your cats. It's late and I'm shot. I need peace, quiet, and sleep, so Bella, get back to the Balis, and Dad, go . . . ah . . . well, go do whatever you were doing before Hurricane Bella dervished in."

The hurricane—a roly-poly vision in skintight black leggings and matching turtleneck top—doled out good-night hugs, then marched on home. Dad began his usual pat down, on the hunt for his reading glasses.

"Dad. Check your nose."

His forgetfulness wasn't funny anymore. Every time I came smack up against it, unease kinked my gut.

He pushed the half-moons up higher on the bridge of his nose, turned to leave the kitchen, paused, and said, "Good night, Haley. And you too, young man."

"Dad! It's Dutch, for goodness' sake. You know, the builder in the paper for the slippery-slope house—"

"Give me a break!" Dutch griped. "That's not all he knows me for. I'm sure you remember me, Reverend. I'm the guy Haley barfed on at the Stokers' home."

"I did not barf on you—"

"Oh." Recognition brightened Dad's eyes. "The one who rowed out to help with Haley's diving instructor that one time. Well, good night, anyway."

Once Dad had left, Dutch turned to me. "Is he all right?"

I shrugged. "You saw what I saw."

"You might want to talk him into a checkup."

"Dad's not the talk-him-into-anything kind, but we'll see." I sighed. "I'd planned to call Doc Cowan to schedule an appointment not so long ago, but I just forgot. I can make the call, but I don't know if I'll be able to talk him into going."

He chuckled. "If you get nowhere, just ask Bella. I'll bet she gets whatever she wants from him. Did you see the sparks fly between them? Phew!"

"Yeah. Gunfire. It's a miracle neither one's full of holes."

"Are you blind, deaf, dumb, and kidding me? That's some hot and heavy chemistry between them."

"Huh? Bella and Dad? Not in this lifetime."

Not even the next.

Dutch made a megaphone of his hands. "Wee-ooh, wee-ooh! Earth to Haley. Wake up and smell the romance."

I went into free fall. My whole world shifted. Dad and Bella? "That's just too bizarre."

Really, really scary.

"I don't think it's weird. But there's lots of funny here." His grin turned wicked. "Gotta love it, Farrell. Your future's bright as . . . oh, let's see. What would Wilmont's favorite designer say?" He thought for a moment, then snapped his fingers. "Sure! Your future's bright as halogen pot lights in the ceiling of life. Picture this: you and the reverend; Bella, your stepmom; and the Balis, stepcats."

I wailed.

He laughed.

It was the perfect way to end a perfectly rotten day.

14

Two days after the battle of bellows in the kitchen, the much-delayed and even more anticipated hand-carved leather and ebonized-wood Guatemalan chairs for Tedd's waiting room arrived. I did the dance of joy when I broke open the first shipping crate.

"Absolute perfection," I burbled at Dutch. "For this office, that is. I'd never stick these in the Weikerts' house or anything like that. But here?" I kissed my bunched-up fingertips. "Mmmuaw!"

"Watch out, Haley. You're going to hurt your shoulder, patting your back like that."

I stuck out my tongue. "Get back to your pile of pick-up-sticks, Builder Boy. I know that's boring, but you made your choice. You grew up to play 'If I Had a Hammer,' while I became the design star."

"Watch it! Your head's so swelled up, it's about to explode all over your nice, new reupholstered chairs."

I did a Bella and slammed my fists on my hips. "What?

229

Are you calling me conceited? You don't think my work's any good? That these chairs aren't faboo for this décor?"

"Lighten up already. I was just joking. You have to cut down on the Starbucks."

"Bite your tongue! It's pure bliss in a cup."

"Ever think what it's done to your stomach lining by now?"

I blinked. "Actually, no. Never." I shrugged. "If my Starbucks and Milky Way bars mean I'm living *la vida loca*, then life as we know it has taken a turn for the dull."

"So in Haley World, you're the last of the daredevil risk takers."

"Oh yeah. For sure. I'm Evel Knievel in drag."

He sputtered, snorted, and laughed. Not some polite chuckle either. He let out a rich belly laugh so contagious that I had to join him.

"That," he said when he could talk again, "is an image to remember. You're absolutely off-the-wall nuts."

I gave him a long look. Then I made both hands into pistols and in a goofy voice said, "Right back atcha, baby."

Dutch shook his head and left, his chuckles so loud that I heard them until he closed the back door. Even though he had too much fun dissing my detective talents, there was a lot to like about the guy. Not the least of which was his sense of humor.

I was in trouble.

I liked him too much.

With a heartfelt sigh, I got back to work. Unveiling the unique chairs felt like a personal triumph. They were incredible in themselves, but when set against the warm, rusticated walls, and once I added the blanket-covered pillows that matched the newly covered meeting-room chairs, they would become absolute masterpieces. As I'd known all along they would.

And because of their perfection, I lost it when I found the final one damaged. The stuffing that gave the tooled backs their fabulous dimension and turned them into 3-D works of art spewed out through a small slit in the leather.

"Aaaarrrgh!"

Okay. So I stomped, screamed, sputtered, and steamed. I griped and whined and contemplated flapping my arms all the way down to a certain Guatemalan artisan studio to confront the careless boob who'd let this happen to one of my beauteous, perfect chairs.

Instead of damage to my arms, I opted for a phone call. Oh, but I did let them have it down in Guatemala. My rage rang out loud and clear; it rang out here in Wilmont. Even Dutch heard it, since he hurried back in, concern on his rugged face.

"Are you all right?"

I nodded, held up a finger, and ended my harangue when the studio owner promised to replace the chair once I returned it.

"Can you believe it?" I asked Dutch. "Look at what they sent me. A torn-up chair, and they charged me 450 bucks for the thing—and it's only four weeks late. Talk about insult to injury."

He checked it out. "Ouch! Bummer. That's amazing work, even if I did tease you earlier."

"Tell me about it." I knelt by the chair and gave the cotton fluff a poke. "I am bummed. But isn't the Trapunto-type work awesome? Look how they stuff with little bits of cotton batting just those areas that are in relief. Can you see how they bring in this stuffing through small slits in the piece of leather that forms the backing? And it comes right up against the carved-out parts. It takes pure genius to do such precise work—"

I gasped. With my pinkie I dug into the slit, parted more of the cotton wadding, and saw what had caught my attention.

"Would you look at that?" I asked.

Dutch drew closer. "What do you see? It looks like a bunch of stuffing to me."

"No, no. Check it out. There, right behind the fluff. Can't you see the shiny glass?"

He pressed the side of his head against mine. Again I didn't pull away. Instead, I welcomed his warmth and closeness.

Crazy, Haley. You are totally, raving nuts.

"Okay," he murmured. "I see what you mean. What do you think? A nail that poked through and tore the leather?"

"Nope. That's not metal. I told you. It's glass."

"I can't see it that well. But glass? Why would there be glass in the backrest of a chair? Can you reach it? Can you pull it out?"

"I'll give it my best."

My tool chest holds all kinds of goodies. I rummaged until I came up with a pair of long, slender steel tweezers. Because I had to return the chair, I couldn't add to the damage. I didn't want the studio owner to blame me for the tear. So little by little I shifted the cotton away from the glass. After a lifetime of sloth-speed minutes, my tweezers slipped around and caught the glass.

"Careful," Dutch whispered. "Don't hurt yourself."

"I'm okay."

I was, until I extracted the stowaway. Once I had it out in the light of day, I fell back on my butt. Dutch drew in a sharp, sibilant breath, more whistle than intake of air.

My tweezers held a rubber-capped glass vial.

Liquid swirled inside.

"Are you thinking what I'm thinking?" I asked Dutch.

"If that's what I think it is, then I'm thinking Tedd's in worse trouble than even you imagined."

A tear rolled down my cheek. "That's what I'm thinking."

"You know what we have to do, don't you?"

Very slowly I pulled myself upright. It felt as if I'd swum through an ocean of mud. "We have to hit the cop shop, and right away."

He ran a long finger across his forehead, then flicked. "Phew! And here I was afraid I'd have to pull a Neanderthal again. You know, throw you over my shoulder and haul you away—this time to jail. To get the evidence to Lila, of course."

It took my all to give him a lame, wimpy smile. "Nah. I'm not that bad. Let's go."

"Your car or mine?"

"Boy, do you live in denial. Your decrepit junk pile is no car. It started life as a pickup truck, and now it's just a massive display of rust."

"It runs."

"Just barely." I grabbed my backpack purse. "Get a move on, Merrill. There's a cop waiting for us. Even though she doesn't know it yet."

We took off in my car. Not a word crossed our lips. I don't know what went through his mind, but I couldn't escape the implications of the vial found in the chair shipped from Central America. Tedd had referred me to the artisan studio.

Tedd was in trouble.

Big time.

And no matter how much I cared, there was no way I could shield her from Lila's radar. At this point my loyalties were split. I'd promised Darlene I wouldn't let her down. I'd also promised to help Cissy prove her innocence. Now a contraband dose of voodoo med implicated one of my closest friends in the murder.

Not a good deal.

In the end one loyalty trumped all others. The Lord called me—all his children—to do justice. It was a no-brainer. I had to see this through; I had to see justice done.

I opened my door. Dutch did the same. I looked his way. Our gazes locked. Compassion glowed in the green.

"You sure you're ready?" he asked.

Before I could stop myself, I answered, "I'm glad you're here."

He slapped the roof of the car. "Then let's rock and roll and get the show on the road."

I crossed the parking lot toward the squatty brick building. At the steps I paused. Dutch reached me, held out his hand. I looked down, then up to his face. That same tenderness I'd seen the night he found me in tears had returned. This time it seemed to hold more significance. I wasn't sure what Dutch wanted from me, but I did know one thing.

If I took his hand today, there'd be no turning back.

Was I ready to take that step?

Where would it lead?

Wimp!

With a quick prayer, I took his hand. We walked in, linked by a warm touch and a shared objective. Dutch is a decent man. He too wanted to see justice done.

Lila met us at her office door. "Let me guess. Tweedle-Dee and Tweedle-Dum. Or is it Tweedle-Dum and Tweedle-Dummer?"

"Cute, Karate Chop Cop." She frowned, and her lips thinned. I waved the vial. "Wait'll you get a load of this."

"What is it?" She gave me her sharpest gimlet look. "Where did you get it? And have you tampered with evidence again?"

I glared. "It's a vial of liquid I found hidden in the stuffing of one of the Guatemalan chairs I ordered for Tedd's office redesign. I haven't tampered with anything. I brought what I found straight to you. And last I checked, this is my civic

duty. Since the vial could be relevant to a murder investigation, I'm here to turn it over to the lead detective on the
case. That's it. Nothing more sinister than that."

She reached for the contraband container. "In a chair you
ordered for Tedd's office."

"Ordered from a studio she recommended."

"I'll have it tested right away."

Dutch cleared his throat. "Will you let us know the results?"

"Would she"—Lila nodded my way—"let me do my
job if I didn't?"

I snorted. "Since when have I kept you from your job—
the one you do so well?"

"You're notorious for your interference—"

"You know what?" Dutch said. "Nature calls, and I'm
tired of your bickering. Go at it all you want, but my blad-
der's more important than your spitting contest."

I watched him walking away, my jaw sagging, my eyes
popping. When I managed to close my mouth and blink
again, I turned to Lila and giggled. Her almond eyes were
opened so wide, they almost looked round. Her jaw gaped,
and I realized what I must have looked like a moment
before.

"He got us," I said.

She shook herself and gave me a tight little smile. "Are
we caught up in a spitting match?"

"I have nothing against you, Miss Perfect. It's just that
painfully perfect perfection that grates on my nerves."

"Me?" She looked stunned. "Perfect?"

Then she snorted. Yeah, her. Wilmont PD homicide detective, Captain Lila Tsu. The most elegant, well spoken, classy . . . I don't know how many other superlatives I could with good reason add to describe Lila's exquisite image.

"That shows how little you know. I'm nowhere near perfect." She glanced at her hands, clasped tight in front of her. "For the record, I'm the one who feels inadequate around you. You're a formidable woman, you know."

I snickered.

I hooted.

I laughed so hard my eyes leaked. "You've got to be kidding, Lila. You're talking about me: Haley Farrell, the klutzy interior designer you say bumbles into your cases and tromps all over your evidence."

"You might be a klutz, and you are too curious for your own good, but you have a rare kind of courage. You also have rock-solid convictions, and you cling tenaciously to them."

"But I—"

"This time you're going to shut up long enough for me to say what I want. Even more than your bravery and strength of conviction, I admire the way you've put your life back together after the rape."

"How'd you know about that?"

"I do have access to all of Wilmont's records, you know. Think I wouldn't check you out? Give me credit for knowing at least a little about police work."

I saw red. "You went digging into my life? Man, are you—"

"I'm a cop, Haley. Remember back when Marge died?

You were the prime suspect. I had to investigate you. And what I found rocked me to the core. You survived a rape and a brutal beating but managed to recover, study martial arts, go back to school, launch your own business, and live a rich life. It takes a unique kind of tenacity, a special woman, to manage all that. You humble me."

My tears flowed. The memories hit me hard. Flashes of fear, pain, rage, grief dug into me. I remembered the struggle to crawl out of the pit of despair where I lived for a time after the rape.

And Lila understood enough to say all that.

"Thanks," I said when I could speak again. "But I had no choice. He didn't kill me. I had to go on and live."

"And you've learned to live well. Precisely my point. Kudos to you, Haley. I mean it from the bottom of my heart."

"Hey! What's up?" Dutch asked. "Why's Haley crying? I leave you two alone for a minute, and I come back to this. Did you accuse her of some monstrous crime again?"

"I'm okay," I said. "Lila said something nice. How rare, huh? So I got mushy and cried."

Lila shrugged. "I called her an admirable woman, and she didn't know how to take it. I'm impressed by the way she's put her life back together. That's all."

Dutch jerked his gaze so fast from the one to the other of us that he must have wound up with whiplash. "This mutual admiration society's too weird for me. And I have to get back to work. You ready, Haley?"

I nodded, still choked up. Who'd a thunk?

When we reached the door, Lila called me. "Don't do anything stupid, okay?"

I rolled my eyes. "Them's fightin' words, Detective Tsu."

"Just let me do my job."

"That you do *so* well," I countered tongue-in-cheek.

I left without a backward look. Dutch and I returned to Tedd's office, and each of us took a dive into our work. I had a million pillows to stuff. He had a gargantuan bookcase to build.

We both had too much to think about.

We didn't talk.

The next day I brought the rest of the artwork I hadn't yet staged around Tedd's office. Since I'd worked last in the meeting room, where I'd left my toolbox, and since the conference table had the largest flat surface in the whole place, I went straight there. The paintings, sculptures, and other Mexican artifacts looked great spread out on the table as a group. They would really shine when I highlighted them one by one.

With some of the items, like the antique carved Mayan chieftain, I'd known where they belonged right from the start. Others, like an amazing handwoven wall hanging in shades of pumpkin, pomegranate, vanilla, and walnut, required a little extra thought.

I walked down the hall and into the waiting room, hanging in hand. I finally decided it belonged in the waiting room, smack dab under one of the small halogen lights I'd had installed around the perimeter of the ceiling. I'd last used the ladder back in the meeting room, so I dragged it out, apologized to the two women and one man waiting to see Tedd, and began to bang the necessary anchors into the faux-adobed drywall.

That's where Dutch found me.

"Here," he said. "You left your cell phone in the meeting room. I answered it when I recognized the number. You're going to want to take this call, but I suggest you come down to solid ground before you do."

Great. His silent message came through loud and clear.

When I heard Lila's voice on the other end, I said, "Wait!" then sent Dutch a grateful look and hurried back to the privacy of the meeting room. He followed and closed the door.

"Okay, Lila. What's up?"

"You wanted the test results on the vial, didn't you?"

"Is Frank Lloyd Wright a genius?"

"I presume that's your way of asking if the sky is blue, only more funky, like you."

"Watch it, Miss Perfect."

"Do you want the results? Then give me a minute to tell you."

Even though the silence threatened to deafen me, I waited her out. I refused to give her another chance at a verbal swipe.

After a long silence, she said, "The vial contains human growth hormone, just as you thought."

I sucked in a sharp breath. There are times when being right is the absolute pits. This was one of those times.

"I'm waiting," Lila said. "When does your 'I told you so' routine start?"

My response came in a simple headshake she'd never see.

Dutch came up from behind, and although he didn't touch me, the warmth radiating from his solid bulk brought me unexpected comfort.

"Very well," Lila went on. "There's more. The serum was tainted—"

"With arsenic."

"Yes, Haley. You're right about that too."

"Is that it now? Or do you have another shoe to drop on me?"

"I'm done dropping shoes."

"Okay. Gotta go. Tons of work. You know how that goes."

"Actually, there is one more thing. Please don't play gumshoe and confront anyone. We don't have enough concrete evidence to do that yet. And you're not the one to do it—ever."

"I'll behave, Karate Chop Cop. I do know how."

"We'll see." And with a truckload of skepticism in her voice, she said good-bye.

When Dutch placed his hands on my shoulders, all my starch and oomph took a hike. I sagged against him and fought hard to pull off a lousy imitation of normal breathing. My stupid stomach revved up to a rollicky rumba.

"I bet you never thought you'd hear me say this," I told

my human crutch, "but being right's not all it's cracked up to be."

"And you're not going to do anything about the vial of poisoned HGH, right?"

"Not directly, no."

He turned me around in his big hands. "Are you out of your freaky, scary, wacko mind?"

"Unfortunately, no. I'm not going to confront anyone with the lab results, but I am going to hold you to that meeting with Ron. Did you ever call him? I want to check out the Weikert brothers, Dr. Dope, the HGH lab and its former owners, the furniture studio that made the chairs—even the agent in Tijuana who markets them. And yes, I want to check out Tedd's business dealings too."

"That I can do. And I called him the night you and I talked."

I grabbed his forearms. "Will you give him another call?"

"Now?"

"Of course now. Why would we want to wait?"

Dutch called Ron, and in minutes we'd agreed to meet at his home within the hour. I hauled my ladder, hammer, anchors, and wall hanging back to the meeting room with a fresh apology for Tedd's two remaining clients.

At the Richardsons', Ron let us in before we had a chance to ring the doorbell. The men shook hands, then wrapped their free arms around each other. Quite different from the first time I came here with Dutch. That time they were bitter enemies bound by old angers and unresolved rivalries. By the grace of God, and after an unspeakable tragedy, they'd rebuilt the friendship they once shared.

Ron's bear hug surprised me. "How've you been, Haley?"

"Same old, same old. Too many houses to beautify, too little time. Too many antiques to sell, too little time."

"I know you're not here to redo our house or sell me something ancient and fabulous, so let's head back to my office."

When I stepped inside the large room, I took a shocked look around. "You're as bad as Larry Weikert!"

Ron gave me a faux angry look. "You owe me an apology, young woman. I work hard for my money."

"Meaning Larry doesn't."

"I could only find a bunch of Internet sales of used electronic equipment and some sporadic consulting jobs. I also tracked down his favorite electronics mart, and when I hinted I might do business with them, the manager didn't balk at my questions. Over the years Larry has dropped close to half a million bucks there."

I goggled. "That buys a lot of wire."

"How did he pay for it?" Dutch asked.

"A couple of times he brought trade-ins. Other times he paid his tab over a period of time. But the bulk of his purchases were cash transactions."

"No wonder Cissy called him a leech." I couldn't get my head around so much money for computers and printers and gadgets of the electronic kind. "I can't believe a smart woman like Darlene shelled out a fortune for . . . for . . ."

Ron shot me a grin. "It takes all kinds, Haley. And the younger one, Tommy, is another mess. He's just stupid when it comes to money. He gets suckered into every bogus scheme that comes down the pike. And his mother paid and paid, until she forced him to settle down. That's when she put up the money for the vintage imports and agreed to pay rent for the showroom and an apartment."

"Aside from how much Larry has sunk into his obsession," I said, "none of this surprises me. I don't suppose you found corpses in their shady pasts."

"That's the extent of the skeletons in their closets. As far as the Mexican doctor goes, he's clean. He has a good credit history, doesn't ever owe much—or at least, not for long—his practice is successful, and he recently invested years of profits in a manufacturing lab. It wasn't enough, and that's why he borrowed money from Darlene Weikert to buy the lab. I also learned he sold his home to pay off the debt, together with funding he arranged from some European pharmaceutical company."

"So money wouldn't be his motive, even if it is a good one for the brothers."

"That's how I see it," Dutch ventured.

I took a deep breath. "What about Cissy?"

"She hit hard times right after she retired. She needed a stent about sixteen months ago. Medicare and her partial supplementary insurance didn't cover everything. She was left with thousands of dollars worth of bills and back rent, and she lost the car she'd bought with a loan. I don't know where she came up with the money, but she paid it all back and then bought an inexpensive used subcompact. She doesn't owe a thing."

My throat closed at the next name. A bullfrog with laryngitis had nothing on me when I asked, "Tedd?"

Dutch wrapped his arm around my waist. I leaned into him.

"She's even cleaner than the others. She's never been a big spender, donates to a number of victims' rights charities, bought her first home three years ago at a government tax sale and paid cash. Aside from a number of flights to Tijuana in the last eighteen months, and they could have been to visit family, there's nothing there."

"Dr. Dope," I murmured. "She was engaged to Dr. Dope."

Ron chuckled. "That's what you call the guy? You're brutal, woman!"

I shrugged. "If the pusher label fits . . ."

"Behave," Dutch said with a squeeze. Then to Ron, "Anything on the previous owners of the lab?"

"The chemist turned seventy-one, neither his son nor daughter was qualified to run the place, and he sold it to Díaz, who'd been one of his regular customers. The guy retired to Acapulco."

I brought my hands palm to palm, then gave a tiny bow. "I'm impressed, Mr. Richardson. You're very, very thorough, even though I have no idea how you got access to that information."

"I aim to please," he said with a grin. "The info is available to me because"—he winked—"I'm no plain old builder, you know. I do some consulting work for the bank on the side—you know, appraising businesses borrowers put up as collateral. Plus, I have access to all kinds of info through my membership in an international consortium of business-men and women."

"He's too modest," Dutch said. "It's an ethics group, and he was just elected president, even though he hasn't been a member for long. Don't think it's a small deal."

Ron blushed. "Had to make up for a lot."

"Never crossed my mind to discount Ron's abilities or accomplishments." Then I sighed. "I have another favor to ask. Maybe you can use your connections to check out an artisan furniture studio in Guatemala."

Ron looked intrigued. "I thought we were dealing with Mexico."

I explained the connection, how the studio sold its pieces through an agent in Mexico—Tijuana, to be exact—how it did a good amount of business with various import/export places in Seattle, and he parked himself in front of a wall of monitors. He typed in a number of pieces of information, frowned, and then typed some more.

We watched him do this a number of times. Each time, his frown grew deeper and his expression more tenacious.

When my curiosity got the better of me, I blabbed. "What's wrong?"

"It's the weirdest thing," Ron said, a bit distracted. "I've found three layers of holding companies, and each one comes back to the good old U.S. of A."

"Can you explain that in any-moron-can-get-it words?" I asked.

"You're no moron," he said, still typing at a fever pitch. "It means that someone has gone to great trouble to hide the owner's identity. A holding company is nothing more than an entity that controls a certain percentage of decision-making votes in another company. Many times they're bogus companies that do nothing much but cloud a trail of shady dealings. In this case, the owners and presidents I've found have names like William Cosby, Theodore Turner, and Lincoln Abraham."

I glanced at Dutch. "Maybe this is it, the connection we were looking for."

"Yeah, but who would it be?"

None of us had even an idea to offer, so Ron got back to his search.

About fifteen minutes later, he said, "Aha!" Dutch and I pressed closer, but then Ron's "no go" deflated our hope. He went on.

After another twenty-five minutes, though, Ron let out a long, shrill whistle. "You are *not* going to believe this. Here. Get a load of this."

He turned the nearest computer monitor so Dutch and I could better see what it showed. I dug my fingers into the hand curved around my waist. We leaned forward.

"No."

"Can't be."

"Read 'em and weep," Ron said. "I can't make it more clear."

The cursor on the screen blinked beside a familiar name.

I took a deep breath and read, "Jacob Weikert."

15

I turned the key in the ignition. "Either someone stole his name, or he's won the Oscars for the next five thousand years."

Dutch slanted me a look. "Do you think that's it? Identity theft? An Alzheimer's patient is an excellent target for that kind of fraud."

My memory kicked in. "Do you remember my close encounter with Larry's moo goo gai pan?"

"You really think I could forget?"

"Well, forget the moo shu pork. *Before* I fell from the tree, Larry was staring at the computers with concentration like Ron's. He seemed . . . I don't know, surprised maybe, or frustrated, by two columns that popped up on one of his screens. He has the expertise to pull off that holding companies scam."

"And he'd have easy access to his father's records."

I flicked my left turn signal and waited for the light. "That's what I think."

"Where are you going? The PD's in the other direction."

"The hospital. If the doctor lets us in, I have some questions for Cissy. She might have seen something that could prove whether or not Larry is the one."

"You're not going to harass an old lady who's had a heart attack, are you?"

"Tommy and Larry are the creeps. Not me."

Out the corner of my eye, I saw him shake his head. So what? I knew Cissy would want to help.

Our patient had been moved to the cardiac care center, a step down from the CICU. I breathed a silent thanks to the Lord. Because of Cissy's upgraded condition, Dutch and I could both visit.

"I wish I'd bought her a balloon or something to celebrate the move," I said.

"You can come back tomorrow, you know."

I grinned. "Okay, Builder Boy. I'll do that. And now we should get this gig going."

After upbeat greetings Dutch and I sat in the available visitor chairs. Before we could say a word, Cissy beat us to the draw.

"What's new?" she asked. "And I don't mean in world markets."

"Go ahead," Dutch murmured.

I took a deep breath. "We've learned the weirdest thing. After enough digging to build us a trench there and back, we learned that the studio where I ordered the handmade Guatemalan chairs is owned by—you won't believe this— Jacob Weikert. And he bought it six months ago."

"That's someone else's Jacob Weikert. Ours can't find his

way to his bedroom, much less to a Guatemalan furniture store."

"I know. But do you think Larry could use his computer skills to pull some kind of scam? He could find his way to Guatemala, Tijuana, or even Timbuktu if he wanted."

"Those two . . ." She set her jaw, compressed her lips, shook her head. "Larry and Tommy are capable of anything. What made you check out the company?"

We told her about the tear in the leather backrest, about the vial, about the tests Lila had run, and then she beat us to the results.

"So that's how the arsenic came," she said. "But did it come here to Wilmont, or did it wind up in Tijuana, where the serums would have been inserted or switched?"

"You used the serum," I countered, "and you're still here. Does arsenic cause heart attacks in people with heart conditions?"

Deep elevens etched in over her brows. "I suppose it could, but I don't think arsenic had anything to do with mine. I've been sick for years, long before I started to take the HGH."

"And Darlene's only taken the serum for about six months."

She nodded and I went on. "You did tell me Jacob didn't take the serum." Another nod. "It makes sense that he wouldn't if he knew it was tainted. But then again, you weren't poisoned, and you took it. So is it possible that Larry could have helped himself to the clean meds you and Darlene bought directly from Dr. Dope—er, Dr. Díaz—and tainted them? With the contraband in the chairs, that is. Did you use the same vial for you and Darlene?"

"No. I used one for me and one for Darlene."

"Where did you keep all this serum?"

"It has to be refrigerated, so we kept it in the kitchen fridge." Then her anger turned to confusion. "Wait! The serum comes in glass ampoules. You have to break off the top at the neck to access the medication."

My excitement fizzled out. "You would have known by a cracked or broken top if someone had messed with the serum."

Nobody spoke for a while. Then Dutch shifted in his seat. I glanced his way and noticed his intense concentration. "What are you thinking?"

He ran a hand through his hair. "Since the serum came in tamperproof all-glass vials, then she must have taken the tainted serum another way."

Cissy *hmphed*. "Darlene wouldn't have injected herself with arsenic. And the serum was the only thing she took by injection."

"Okay," Dutch said. "How about this? What if she took the serum thinking it was something else?"

"You mean like in water or food?"

"Maybe with another medication."

"It was the only injection she took—"

"I got it!" I grabbed my chair's steel arms. I felt dizzy from the many different pictures that clicked through my mind. "Maybe he injected a pill. What else did she take, and where did you keep it?"

"I kept their medications in a steel cabinet in the upstairs linen closet. Darlene took a dozen prescriptions each day, from cancer treatment drugs to sleeping pills at night. But you can't inject the serum into a capsule or a tablet. It would melt."

"That's it! That's really, really it! The sleeping pills. That's how he did it."

"But I just said you couldn't add serum to the pills—"

"No, no. I got that. He shot her up *after* she took her sleep meds, once she was so zonked she wouldn't notice the needle stick. That's how he got it in her. And he used the serum from the different vials, the ones he snuck in on his own. No one would think twice of a needle puncture in Darlene. She must have been a medicine pincushion if you were giving her regular HGH shots."

Even though it was somewhat of a stretch given how little actual evidence we had, I was sure I'd figured it out. When I scared up the guts to look at Dutch, I saw acceptance dawn on his face. Cissy's eyes had opened wider, and a slow smile curved her lips.

"So?" I asked.

Dutch stood and held out a hand. "We might not have all the dots connected yet, but I think this is the right track. I want to get back to Ron's. We need to track the chairs. You know, where they're shipped, who buys them, do they always go to Tijuana, or do they come straight here? And which import stores buy them on a regular basis."

I took his hand. "I ordered the ones for Tedd's office right from the artisan studio in Guatemala, but I also spoke with the agent in Tijuana. They were the ones who would ship them here. The delay in our shipment is supposed to have happened in Guatemala, not in Tijuana. I had to make a bunch of frustrating calls down there to shake them loose." We headed for the door. "I'll go check with Tedd while you and Ron do your thing. We have to find out where Tedd learned about the chairs. And she needs to know what we found out about Larry."

"We're not sure it was Larry who set up the fake companies," Cissy, the voice of reason, said. "Someone else who steals identities could have done it."

"True," I said. "But I think we're onto something here. And it's the serum that clinches it. Larry has the knowledge and the computer equipment to pull it off, plus he had the access to Darlene and her medication." I leaned over Cissy to give her a careful hug. "Keep up the good work, Mrs. Star Patient. Hurry up and get well. I'll see you tomorrow."

Dutch and I hurried to the car. "Don't you think you should let your alter ego in on the scoop?" he asked.

"I guess you mean Lila."

"Who else?"

So I did like a good girl and called the detective diva. In less than five minutes, I'd brought her up to speed on what Ron had learned and what Cissy had told us. Aside from a couple of "I sees" and two or three "reallys?" Lila kept her peace until I finished.

"I won't even ask how you got into credit records, financial statements, sales transactions—whatever you tapped into. But I will admit you were thorough. And now it's

time for you to back off. We'll continue to follow the av-
enues we've been following, and you will go back to your
redesign."

"But—"

"Want to be my guest again?"

I shuddered. "Fine. I'm on my way to Tedd's anyway. I
owe her an apology."

"Not so fast, Haley. Don't discuss this with her—with
anyone. And whatever you do, don't do anything stupid.
I really don't want to lock you up again."

I blew a curl off my forehead. "A word to the wise and
all that, Lila. I get your point. Just make sure you get the
guy."

"Someday you'll figure it out. I don't need you to do
my job."

I didn't dignify that comment with a response. We drove
to Tedd's, where Dutch got into his trashed truck and
headed back to Ron's house.

In the office, Willa told me Tedd had gone to a lunch
meeting, so I decided to come back later, closer to when
she'd finish her last appointment. I still had the Rockies,
the Andes, and the Alps living on my desk.

The wait—for Dutch to call with a Ron update and for
Lila to tell me the chairs' trail had led straight to Larry's
now braceleted wrists—kept me in an altered state. Well,
altered in that I was twitchier than a toddler and jumpier
than a pogo stick.

I know I'm impatient, but I think I exhibited a superlative
abundance of patience. I did wait until late afternoon.

But as soon as my office clock read 5:45, I was gone. I raced to Tedd's and arrived within a couple of minutes.

Willa had told me earlier that Tedd's last appointment ended at a quarter to five, and I know from experience that even though Willa leaves for class as soon as the last client walks out, Tedd stays until six or seven.

I should have paid more attention to the unlocked back door. But I blame my distraction on my impatience. At least I didn't barrel in like I normally would have; I was uncertain of Tedd's welcome after all I'd said.

My hesitation let me catch the murmur of words. I heard a man and a woman talking in the waiting room, and while I couldn't catch their actual words, I got the general gist of their argument. The male voice broadcast his anger, demand, and persistence and cut off Tedd every time she spoke.

Her voice remained even and soothing. But the little hairs on the back of my neck prickled up to attention. Something wasn't copacetic here. I knew that professional voice; it's the one she uses to keep her clients calm.

Tedd was in danger. And because of the way my mind works, with every passing second I grew more certain of one thing: this was about Darlene Weikert.

Should I turn around and get us help? That would leave Tedd alone with . . . Larry?

Should I instead make my way closer to the waiting room, get a grip on the situation, and then help Tedd before Larry could hurt her? Could I do it alone?

I thought of my cell phone. Under cover of a somewhat

louder outburst, I hit the speed dial. When Dutch answered I stepped closer to Tedd and Larry. I prayed Dutch would hear the disagreement; Larry's voice grew louder by the minute.

When Dutch stopped barking his greeting but didn't hang up, I figured he'd heard. I moved a tiny ways forward; set the phone down on the hall floor; prayed for strength, courage, and wisdom; and pushed myself tight against the wall. Inch by inch I drew closer to the waiting room, where Larry got madder by the second.

When I finally took a peek into the room, what I saw shook me to the core. The impossible, incomprehensible, inconceivable unfolded before my eyes.

It wasn't Larry with Tedd in the waiting room.

A very angry but very lucid Jacob Weikert held a gun to Tedd's head. "Sign!" he yelled. "You can't change what's happened or what's about to happen, so do what you know you have to do."

"Why did you pretend an illness like Alzheimer's?" Tedd asked, her patience and serenity admirable even though her hands wore tight grey-duct-tape bracelets.

He answered with a nasty laugh. "Because nobody expects anything of you, so you can finally do whatever you want. You're just the dummy in the corner. And now that you know, sign!"

"Why are you going to the trouble to make it look like I killed myself? Wouldn't it be easier if it just looks as though someone broke in? A robbery or something?"

"That doesn't take care of Darlene. Enough with your

questions. That's all you ever do, ask, ask, ask! Sign the suicide letter so we can be done with this."

Tedd blanched, but she didn't falter. "I'm curious about another thing," she said. "Why did you hurt—kill—Darlene? She loved you."

"Don't you ever stop with the questions? Will you sign if I answer this last one?" Once Tedd nodded, he said, "I got tired of Darlene holding the purse strings, so I figured out a way to make my own cash. Artsy junk from Central America sells great, and the HGH does even better. There's a world of money to be made off sickos. Besides, it suits me to wind up a widower with a horrible disease. No one's ever going to know what I did."

I'd heard enough. A long step brought me to within fifteen feet of the man. "I don't think so, Jacob. I know, Tedd knows, and the PD now knows too."

I hoped.

He spun toward me and gave me the break I needed. I raised my hands into position, spun two preparatory turns, and with my left foot smashed his gun hand.

A bullet shattered a window.

The gun flew across the room.

Another shot erupted, and the bullet lodged into the wall.

Jacob screamed.

Adrenaline pumped through me. I focused on my opponent and, with the outside edge of my right hand, landed a blow a few inches to the right of his neck. The *crunch* was followed with Jacob's inhuman cry. He fell to the ground,

his right side now useless because of the broken collar-
bone.

"Thank you, Father," I murmured. "And thank you too,
Tyler Colby, *sensei* extraordinaire."

"Impressive," Tedd said.

"I can chop and kick with the best of them, but I'm sorry
I didn't figure out whodunit before Jacob did this to you."
I pulled off my backpack purse and extracted my embroidery scissors from the bottom of that portable pit. "These
are killer, you know? I use them all the time."

She rubbed her wrists once I'd snipped through the tape.
"And never for counted cross-stitch either."

"Preach it, sister, preach it!"

I turned to Jacob, who was moaning where he'd fallen.

I turned back to Tedd. "Any more of that duct tape?"

She stood and headed for the couch. I blocked her way.
"Go back and sit. Tell me where to find the universal fix
all. Our misguided Sir Lawrence Olivier didn't terrorize
me. What a waste of talent. Think what Jacob might have
become if he'd auditioned for a movie or two instead of
concocting this insane plot to kill his wife."

The front door burst open. "Hands up. I got a gun!"

Tedd and I gaped at a female who'd hijacked Bella's
voice, whose face was unrecognizable beneath black grease-
paint smears, whose body's generous rolls were stuffed into
familiar black leggings and a turtleneck top.

I really, really didn't want it to be her. "Bella?"

"You okay, Haley girl? Did I get here in time?"

"In time for what? To be dragged off to the loony bin?

What were you thinking, woman? Put that gun down before you hurt yourself or anyone else."

Bella's blue eyes peered out from the sea of shiny black goo. "In the first place," she said in a haughty tone, "I'm da bomber with a gun—that's hip talk for really, really good. And in the second place, what you see here is my authentic reproduction imitation pistol from the Virtual University of Possum Bend, Connecticut. That's my alma's mortar. The gun's to help you fake out the bad guys while you wait for cops to show up. It doesn't shoot or anything. Isn't that clever?"

Somehow a showdown with a killer, armed with a not-a-gun gun, didn't strike me as all that smart. But who am I to say?

And before I did say anything, I noticed Jacob's attempts to rise. "No, you don't, buddy."

"Oh boy," Bella said. "He's the bad guy? And he thinks he's gonna split? No way, Jose!"

She marched straight to Jacob, shoved him facedown, and then parked her abundant behind on the back of his knees. "Let's see him try and get away now."

Jacob yowled at the audacious affront.

"Are you okay?" Dutch yelled from the open front door.

Even though the threat to Tedd and me was under control—or under Bella, to be more precise—relief swept through me. "A little late this time, Builder Boy. Of course I'm okay. So are Tedd and Bella."

He glanced at Wilmont's pet detective. "Why's she here?"

Bella gave him the evil eye. "What do you think? I came to save Haley. I'm the calgary—"

"Cavalry," I said automatically.

"Whatever. I followed her so I could come to her rescue and bring up the rear. Can't you see I'm overpowering the perp?"

Dutch's eyes widened. "Is that . . . ?"

"Allow me to introduce Jacob Weikert," I said, "wife killer, con artist, drug smuggler, fraud expert, Oscar-worthy actor, and all-around creep."

The creep made a series of noises I couldn't translate. He also bucked, but Bella gave a whoop and smacked one of his legs with her faux gun.

"Did you call Lila?" I asked Dutch.

"The minute I figured out what was coming down."

"She's taking her sweet time, then."

"Who's taking her sweet time?" the detective asked. "And what happened here?"

I gestured for Tedd to explain, and Dutch came to stand at my side. "Thanks," I murmured. Then the shivers began for real.

"I should have been here with you." Then he narrowed his eyes. "You want to take back that 'I'm okay' you fed me?"

My chattering teeth made it hard to get the words out, but I persevered. "How about I say I was okay when I answered?"

He slipped behind me, wrapped both arms around me, and pulled me close. I took a shuddery breath and leaned back against him, glad for his solid bulk, his gentle strength, his care and compassion, his presence at my side.

Was I in trouble or what?

"I'll buy that, but it is kind of a letdown. I figured I'd pluck you from the jaws of death again, do my knight-on-the-white-horse act, swoop you up, and cart you out of harm's way."

I looked him in the eye. Mischief sparkled there. "Tell you what, Builder Boy. You keep your handy-dandy little phone charged all the time, and I'll call you in to save the day the next time I need you."

He shook his head. "You're a piece of work, you know?"

"And you're a pain—over and over again. But who's counting?"

"We're heading out now," Lila said. "But be prepared. I'll have questions for you after I get him booked."

"I'm ready," I said.

She smiled. "When aren't you?"

As Chris Thomas walked past Lila, his hand a manacle on Jacob's arm, he looked back to Dutch and me. "When she should see what's right before her nose. I know I'm out of the game, but I do hope you wind up the winner, Haley. Be happy."

I blushed and tried to escape Dutch's embrace. I got nowhere.

Bella tucked her faux pistol into the elastic waistband of her leggings. "Yeah, fine. So I got to sit on the jerk. How come you didn't call me, Haley? I'm the one with the license to grill—the crook, that is. That's what we in the business call putting the bad guys on the hot seat."

I felt Dutch's silent laughter against my back and struggled to keep mine inside. "Ah . . . well, you see . . . oh yeah! I just hit the button that calls the last number dialed, and it turned out to be Dutch."

She narrowed her blue eyes. "You sure?"

Dutch and I nodded.

Tedd grinned.

Bella shrugged. "I'm still bummed. I missed all the fun trying to find a parking spot." She turned to Tedd. "Did you see how full your lot is tonight? What's up with that? Is someone having a twofer sale?"

Tedd tried to look serious and, for the most part, succeeded. "Not exactly, Bella. Tonight's the monthly meeting of the Wilmont Rock Hound Club. Those are their cars."

She wrinkled her nose. "Rock hound? Never heard of that dog breed. What do they look like? Do they get along with cats? Think the Balis would like one? Or maybe Midas wants a pal."

That did it. We laughed until I cried. Tedd hurried off to the bathroom down the hall, her giggles tinged with a touch of hysteria—our extreme responses understandable after what we'd just gone through. Dutch stopped and started, each time his chuckles heartier than before.

Bella? She just glared.

"Where's the joke? What's so funny?"

That sent Dutch into another fit of laughter, so it fell on me to explain. "Rock hounds aren't dogs. They're people who're into stones. They collect them, identify them—kind of like stamps, only heavier and probably dirtier too."

"That's it?" Her disappointment showed through the war paint.

Tedd walked back into the room. "That's not all." She held out a wad of tissues. I took some to wipe my eyes, but the woman under the black goo didn't even notice my shrink's offering.

Tedd went on. "Yes, they do collect regular rocks, but most of them collect gems. Anything from diamonds to garnets to sapphires and tanzanite too. You should see some of their finds."

Bella tipped her head to a side. "That's kinda cool . . . I think. I could use some new jewelry. Maybe I'll get on over there and check 'em out for myself."

Before I could stop her rush toward disaster, she was gone. I winced. "Oh, pity those poor innocent geologists and gemologists next door. Hurricane Bella's on her way."

Tedd grinned. "Pity the PD when they realize she's the rock hounds' cat burglar . . . or maybe she'd say 'cat bungler.' But she's not that bad, Haley. I hope I'm still that lively and alert when I'm her age. And remember what I told you. A December romance would take care of a lot of Bella's quirkier traits. So how have your matchmaking efforts been?"

Dutch laughed again.

I spun and poked a finger into his chest. "Not a word, Merrill. Not a word."

"What's the problem?" Tedd asked.

Dutch hummed the *Fiddler on the Roof* tune and raised his hands in surrender, wicked glee all over his face. "Matchmaker, here, doesn't have to do much to fix Bella up. There's romance in our favorite pet detective's future. And Haley's part of that future. Smokey the Bear has to watch out for our Bella. You can set off a forest fire with the sparks between her and Reverend Hale."

Tedd's alarm rivaled my horror.

"Yup," Dutch added. "Haley's future is rosy, all right. She gets Bella for a stepmom and even the Balis for stepcats."

I stomped out the back door and down to the parking lot, turned the key in the Honda's ignition, and went home to bed. My nightmares were ripe. They featured Bella, the Balis, litter boxes, and me.

And to think I'd entertained the momentary delusion of a date with the jerk.

No way. No how.

Not in a million years.

Dutch Merrill was nothing more than a pain. A necessary evil on the path to my career success. But that was all.

So why did I feel so bummed out?

Epilogue

I got over my snit soon enough. I'd been at Tedd's, steaming the creases out of the custom curtains, when a call from the clinic summoned me to Cissy's bedside. Her condition had deteriorated without warning. Dutch took one look at my teary face, confiscated the Honda keys, and got us there in minutes and in one piece.

We arrived in time for me to hold Cissy's hand, join her in prayer, and then see her draw her last breath, a peaceful smile on her lips.

Dutch knelt at my side, his arm around my shoulders. I cried, my tears half sad, half grateful. "What a difference a few weeks and a meeting with the Father makes," I finally said.

"Meaning . . . ?"

"That when I first met her, if you'll remember, she wanted the HGH to be the fountain of youth because she was so scared of death. Today she went home to the Lord in peace—she was even smiling. God's still in the miracle business."

"And I'll bet you had everything to do with helping that miracle along."

"All I did was tell her what I know and then pray for her. I wish I could help miracles happen. I'm afraid I need a big one right about now."

A frown drew his brows together. "What's wrong?"

"Nothing with me. But you saw my dad. Something's not right there. And I'm scared . . ."

His gaze scoured my face. "Alzheimer's."

A new flood fell from my eyes. "In a nutshell. He's become so forgetful lately . . . I don't know what to say."

"Don't say anything." He gave me a squeeze. "Get him to a doctor. You can even ask Tedd for a referral. I bet she knows a number of good specialists."

I blinked. "Why didn't I think of that? I made an appointment with Doc Cowan, but a referral from Tedd makes a lot of sense."

"You're too close, Haley. He's your father, and you only want to see good things." He slipped a finger under my chin. "No matter what happens, I just want you to know I'm here for you. You can lean on me anytime. I'll be right behind you. All you have to do is reach out."

My stomach flipped, and my heart took flight. But then I unfurled a net of common sense to catch it and bring it back to my control. I couldn't give the emotion of the moment the upper hand.

"Thanks." I covered his fingers with mine. "I mean it,

Dutch. I do appreciate your offer." I stood. "But we'd better call a nurse. They need to see to Cissy."

"I think," he said as he drew to his full height, "God's seen to Cissy by now. Let's go see to your dad."

We left the clinic hand in hand.

A week later I looked in my full-length mirror and didn't recognize the woman there. After years of plain T-shirts and soft, casual long skirts, I'd taken the leap and gone shopping. The results looked good.

I looked good.

The ivory silk blouse's lines paid homage to the classic tailored men's shirt. But its extra-wide, decorative lapels and the fabric's rich buttery sheen were nothing short of feminine glam. The wide V opening at the neck showcased my mother's beautiful strand of pearls to perfection.

But that wasn't the most remarkable part of my outfit. My skirt—short for me—skimmed the knees, its yummy caramel color made more beautiful by the drape of the whisper-fine cashmere. And for a touch of the unexpected, I'd added a ribbon belt that closed in a flirty bow and tails. The color? The exact same shade as Dutch's green eyes.

Why?

Because I'm crazy.

Insane. Stark raving nuts.

And because I was waiting for Builder Boy to pick me up for our date. Our first date—the first, as he said, of many, many more to come.

Butterflies? Yeah right. My gut lurched and bucked at

the 757s crash-landing in there. And he expected me to eat?

Then the doorbell rang, and I had no more time to beat myself up. I went to dinner with Dutch, *not* at a certain Thai restaurant either. He took me to the most elegant place I'd ever seen—even in one of my much-loved vintage films. The menu was a single crisp sheet of translucent parchment with only five entrée selections. But what selections they were!

Filet mignon . . . lobster tails . . . truffled duck . . .

Of course, the prices were a well-kept secret. And my date was the builder who'd nearly gone under. Why would he want to spend so much money? I'd have been just as happy, and probably more comfortable, at the Golden Arches or the nearest diner that served perfect fries.

"Are you sure you want to pay this much for just a dinner?"

The green eyes glittered, and he crossed his arms. "Don't you think it's time to celebrate?"

"Celebrate? What are we celebrating?"

"Our imminent merger, of course."

My stomach flipped. "Huh?"

Sure. My infamous eloquence always shows up at the worst possible time. But what can I say? He'd left me speechless.

"I look at it this way. You're the best designer in Wilmont—"

"The *only* designer in Wilmont."

He shrugged. "That still makes you the best, right?" Once

I rolled my eyes and nodded, he went on. "And I've begun to build a new base of operations in Wilmont instead of Seattle proper, so it only makes sense for us to join forces and offer our clients a full-service, one-stop-shopping experience for their homes and offices."

To my dismay, I couldn't argue with his logic. He's a whiz with a hammer and nails, hires exceptional subcontractors, brings projects in under budget and on time if not sooner, tends to solve problems with the greatest of ease, and by now knows all my quirks and eccentricities.

"I can see where that could work," I said. "Certainly for me. But what's in it for you?"

"You have to ask? You're the most notorious designer in the country—aside from the ones on TV. With you on my team, people are going to knock down the door just to get a look at the killer decorator."

Even though he said it with a straight face, he did wink.

"I'm going to do you a favor, Merrill. I'm going to ignore what you just said. But you might have a good idea there—for once."

"So it's a deal. Merrill and Farrell for the Home is a go."

I hooted. The other patrons of the chichi restaurant turned to stare. I glared. They returned to their din din, and I to my ding-dong.

"In your dreams, Builder Boy. It's Farrell and Merrill for the Home, or it's a no go."

His look sent ripples of excitement through me. "That'll do. For now."

"Wha—" I had to clear my suddenly clogged throat to go on. "What do you mean, for now?"

He reached across the table and took my hand in his. "I'm interested in way more than a business merger, Haley. I'm interested in you. How about it? Want to see if that merger's in our future too?"

I gulped. The moment had come. As I'd known it would. I'd thought I was ready, but I'd thought wrong.

"Um . . . I don't know what to say. I mean, I do like you, Dutch, but a romance?" Tears filled my eyes at the disappointment in his. "Remember when I told you I'm Tedd's client and not just her friend?"

He nodded but didn't speak.

"There's a lot I have to tell you, but this isn't the place. For now I have to say no, no romance. My faith isn't that strong. Yet."

His trademark stubbornness put in its appearance in his squared jaw, his intense green stare, the subtle tightening of his hold on my hands.

When I didn't pull away, he smiled. It was his mischievous smile, the one that always melted away a chunk of my defense.

"I'm taking that 'yet' of yours as a promise, Haley Farrell. And I'll hold you to that story you owe me too. But there's no rush here. I'm staying right at your side. I'll wait for you."

Hope fluttered back to life. "You do that."

He studied me for a long time, as if looking for an answer on my features but finding none. "What are you going to do about your snooping addiction? Have you thought about joining the PD? Getting a degree in law enforcement?"

I considered smacking him for all of a second. Then, in the interest of amicable business relations, I shook my head. "You're not the only one to bring it up. But that's not me. I'm happy with my career. Careers. Don't forget the auction house I also have to run."

He raised his brows. "You're telling me you plan to be too busy in the future? Does that mean you're done snooping? I won't have to deal with any more 'I can do better than Lila' stunts?"

"You're no slouch in the detecting department yourself."

"I just follow in your wake, Hurricane Haley. I don't go out of my way to find murders to solve."

No way would I dignify that with a response. Instead, I said, "I can promise I won't look for reasons to snoop. But I can't control what I'll face along the way. Only God can see my future, and all I can do is trust in him."

Dutch dropped back into his chair, an almost comical grimace on his face. "I'm in trouble, aren't I?"

I shrugged.

"Well, Farrell. The way I see it, I have only one choice. I better start to pray."

Ginny Aiken, a former newspaper reporter, lives in Pennsylvania with her engineer husband and their three younger sons—the oldest is married and has flown the coop. Born in Havana, Cuba, and raised in Valencia and Caracas, Venezuela, she discovered books at an early age. She wrote her first novel at age fifteen while she trained with the Ballets de Caracas, later to be known as the Venezuelan National Ballet. She burned that tome when she turned a "mature" sixteen. An eclectic list of jobs, including stints as reporter, paralegal, choreographer, language teacher, retail salesperson, wife, mother of four boys, and herder of their numerous and assorted friends, including the 135 members of the Crossmen Drum and Bugle Corps, brought her back to books in search of her sanity. She is now the author of twenty-three published works, but she hasn't caught up with that elusive sanity yet.